ALPHA CLASS 03: DISCOVERY

ALPHA CLASS 03: DISCOVERY

ETHERIC ACADEMY

TS PAUL   ND ROBERTS   MICHAEL ANDERLE

LMBPN

DISRUPTIVE IMAGINATION

LMBPN Publishing
PMB 196, 2540 South Maryland Pkwy
Las Vegas, NV 89109

First US edition, March 2020

CHAPTER ONE

United Kingdom, North Wales, Undisclosed Location

The door of the sterile room opened. The woman twisted her wrists, attempting to relieve the pinch of the cable ties holding them to a metal loop embedded in the tabletop. She looked up, meeting the expectant stares of the sharply dressed men as they took the chairs in front of her, one at a time.

Her eyes narrowed. "Do you scumbags know who I work for? You're going to be in a world of hurt when my bosses find out you've taken me!" She worked her wrists one more time for good measure.

And got nowhere.

The man to her left gave a brief, brittle smile. "Don't worry, Doctor Llewellyn. You are only scheduled for a short visit. It is your position at TQB Enterprises that drew our attention to you."

The second man took a sheaf of papers from his briefcase and passed it to the first, who shuffled them, looking for something. "Ah, there we are. Doctor Laura Llewellyn. Early graduation from university, straight into a research position. Stayed there until your radical thesis on isostatic pressing interested TQB enough that they bought you a castle." He looked up at her. "Is all of that correct?"

She pulled against the ties on her wrists again, to no avail. "Do you know my underwear size as well? Creepy little man—that's what you are. Let. Me. *Go!* I'll report you to the authorities, I will! You won't get away with this!"

"We *are* the authorities, Doctor Llewellyn." The man smiled blandly. He reached into the inside pocket of his jacket and pulled out his wallet to show her his identification. There was an MI5 watermark in the background.

He leaned forward just a touch. "You see, we are working on behalf of Her Majesty's government. You are in the position to assist us in a matter of vital national importance. This will all go away in an instant if you get us what we need to make the TQB armor you've been working on."

The man—Agent Broadbent—put his wallet away and straightened up. "What will it be, Doctor? Will you do the right thing?"

"That's *not* the right thing, and no, I *won't* do it. TQB has been good to this nation—especially here in North Wales— and I won't betray them!" Her eyes narrowed in defiance and her mouth pursed in an angry grimace. "Anyone can fake a badge. You can go to Hell, the lot of you!"

Broadbent tutted and shook his head. His face was sad as he took a smartphone out of his immaculate suit jacket. He sent a message, then pulled up a video with a couple of swipes and held it out for her to see.

She gasped when she saw her husband and two children being shoved roughly into a scruffy Ford Transit van by more suited agents. "What have you done? You stupid man, you've made the worst mistake of your life! Do you not watch the news? Don't you know what happens to people who use children as leverage against TQB?" She struggled to free herself once more, trying her damndest to attack the agents. "You're dead men walking, you are. Let my family go!"

Broadbent shook his head. "Doctor Llewellyn, you have put me in a difficult position. I was hoping we could avoid such nastiness, but your lack of cooperation has given me no choice." He put the phone away. "Look, I don't want to have to do this. Using innocent citizens as leverage is beyond the pale, but my bosses want those specs. These are frightening times, Laura. May I call you Laura? You must know what is happening in the wider world. War is everywhere, and it will reach our shores soon enough. We need that armor, and its weapons to keep our people safe." He leaned in, placing a hand atop hers. "England needs you."

Laura pulled her hand away quickly, ignoring the bite of the ties when she jerked them tight. "I don't give a damn about what England needs. England sure as hell doesn't give a crap about Wales! What have you done to my family? Where have you taken them?" She strained against her restraints, spitting mad.

Broadbent sat rigidly in his chair, his face stony. "Histrionics will get you nowhere, Doctor Llewellyn. Why not just do as I ask? Then your family goes free and we forget about all this unpleasantness." He waved at her. "The nation will be indebted to you for your service. Doesn't that sound nice?"

She shook her head resolutely. "No, it doesn't. It sounds like the biggest pile of horse crap I've ever heard." She sighed heavily. "Even if I wanted to help you, I can't do it. It's not my department!" she finished, her voice just a touch less strident.

"Doctor Llewellyn, if you do not comply, I assure you that the consequences for your family will not be pleasant. See?" Broadbent took out his phone and displayed the video stream again. Laura repressed a sob at the sight of her children crying in their father's arms. They were huddled together in the back of the dirty van, shell-shocked and afraid. "Just do as we ask. Then they go free."

Laura's head dropped in defeat. "If I get caught I'm sending them straight to you! My family..." she asked, jerking her chin at the phone. "Where are you taking them? You'd better not hurt them!"

The other man spoke. "They are safe—for now. But you understand what's at stake here, Doctor Llewellyn: if you do not do as we ask, if you speak to anyone at TQB about our little chat, I will be delivering much sadder news. Her Majesty *must* have Gauntlet."

CHAPTER TWO

BBS *Meredith Reynolds*, Earth Orbit

Q Diane and Dorene pored over the schedules for the umpteenth time. Dorene stamped her foot in frustration. "They start in two days, and we still haven't gotten the assignments pinned down! Whose idea was it to mess with the class schedules?"

Diane looked up. "I believe it was yours, DJ." She patted Dorene's hand. "It's going to be worth the hassle. The competition for a spot in one of the two fighter pilot groups this term was one of your best ideas yet! The kids took their skills to the next level to try and win a place." She took a second to smooth her braid, catching a loose strand and tucking it in while she stared at the roster on the desk. "Look at Todd Grimes' scores. He's going to be one of our best pilots when he grows up. We knew it would cause problems this term, so we just have to suck it up."

Dorene cheered up at that. "You're right, dear. I was

speaking to one of the fighter boys last week. Thomas, his name was—nice young man with *such* a cute…"

Diane arched an eyebrow.

Dorene hid her laugh with a cough. "He told me that the students' training tactics are being added to the play-book as fast as the kids come up with them." She took a sip of the cooling coffee on her desk and set it down again with a grimace. "Ugh. Aleksi from Delta is applying his skills in statistics to the planning of the gaming events now. He's got the whole thing running as smooth as silk."

Diane agreed, "It's getting competitive! The top ten deserve to get specialist training, and increasing their knowledge base can only help them improve on what they're already achieving. But it is going to be a total night-mare for the scheduled core classes. Our faculty are extending themselves to fit the classes into their schedules as it is. They don't have the *time* to repeat the class when the fighter groups are done. Those students will have missed out. We can't have that, DJ."

Diane's brow furrowed in thought. "It's a good idea, we're just not thinking big enough." She began tapping on her tablet and muttered, "I have the solution. There's already one group specializing this term, so why not go the whole hog and send each student to the place they're likely to end up when they graduate? We have their aptitude scores from the entrance exams, and we can use those to build a list of skillsets and assign a mentor to each."

Dorene stared open-mouthed at her twin for a moment as the idea sank in. "That's…*genius*. We split *all* the classes, sharpening the individual students and strengthening the teams overall in the process. Then no student misses out on the core skills."

She began making a new list.

Diane dropped her tablet on the desk with a flourish. "I've just sent a memo to all department heads, telling them their future replacements are coming to spend the next six weeks learning from them."

The two just looked at each other for a moment, imagining what the teachers would do when they got *that* email, then burst into laughter.

Diane wiped a tear from her eye. "Let's arrange it all before the conscripted mentors descend on us. If we're going to create chaos, let it be *organized* chaos!"

CHAPTER THREE

Q BBS *Meredith Reynolds,* **Alpha Class Dormitory**

There were mixed feelings in the Alpha class dorm.

The kids surrounded Nestor, who would be leaving them for the pilot's barracks, and Maxim, who would be staying with the Guardian recruits. Their separate assignments had come as a shock to the Wechselbalg cousins, Maxim especially. He and Nestor were closer than brothers, and had expected to get into the fighter group together. None of the kids wanted to be separated from the rest of their team.

Maxim was grumbling as he packed his belongings.

As always, Yana took charge. "Cheer up," she said stoically. "It is only for six weeks. You get to stay with the Guardians, and John Grimes will be your mentor, Maxim. *John Grimes!*" She sighed wistfully at the thought of the Queen's Right Hand.

Maxim blushed. "It is good, *da*. I will be learning from the best. It is honor to me—and to my father—to be

9

chosen. But I will miss my brother from another mother." He squeezed Nestor's shoulder.

"I agree with Yana. Six weeks is not long to be apart," Nestor declared. "I am almost a little jealous you get to take advanced combat with him, but I will become an ace pilot. So like you say, is good."

Tina giggled and pretended to gag. "All right, give it a rest. It's weird seeing you people swoon over John. Who did you get, Yana?"

Yana's regal face brightened when she tapped her tablet to reveal her own assignment. "I have been placed with your mother to learn leadership and management skills. How wonderful! What about you? You too, Ron...who did you get?"

"Jean Dukes," they said at the same time. It was their turn to blush. The whole team erupted into fits of giggles.

"Oooh, our lovebirds get to stay together!" Yana trilled.

Ron spluttered, his face turned beet-red, and he made a big deal of looking at his tablet screen. Tina laughed Yana's teasing off. It was an open secret that she and Ron had become close—especially since the meeting of their minds now turned into a meeting of their lips whenever the adults weren't looking.

Ron looked up from his tablet, embarrassment forgotten. "Jean's class is going to be *awesome*. Look here—planning and application of resources, bootstrapping, the practical applications of engineering. Wait, that can't be right... There's no PT anywhere on my schedule. I *love* this school!"

"What?" Yana held her hand out for Ron's tablet. "No way!" She checked her own after confirming it was true. "I have regular training scheduled. I'm going to miss being with you all so much. I haven't made many friends outside our team."

"You could always request to come with us," Tina said.

Yana shook her head. "No. Who would take care of Bai Hu if I went to the other side of the station? You know he'll only let me or Guardian Commander Silvers near him. He needs me. Besides, I'm looking forward to a quiet time aboard the *Meredith Reynolds*, no adventure for me! It was scary being shot at by the Mongolian and Chinese armies, and it was worse not being able to fight back. I need time to train."

"I'll come train with you, even though I get a pass too," Tina offered. "If I have time, that is. It's weird that we get a pass when the administrators have just put all the new fitness requirements in place. How are we going to meet them if we don't train?"

"What if it's because Ms. Dukes will have us doing hard labor in the R&D labs?" Ron piped up from across the room, where he was pulling his shoes out of his locker. "You know that her R&D department is in charge of transforming all the stuff BMW comes up with into reality.

Yana interjected, "We'd better get going, or we'll be late for breakfast."

They all agreed on that, grabbing their tablets and exiting the dorm in a noisy rush.

QBBS *Meredith Reynolds*, Etheric Academy Cafeteria

The cafeteria was abuzz with the murmurs of the

students discussing their individual assignments over breakfast.

Craig and Halli from Bravo came over and sat at the Alpha table across from Maxim, and the older boy leaned forward. "Hey, Maxim, we heard you got John Grimes."

Maxim grinned. "You heard right."

"The Kosolov twins are with us as well," Halli revealed. "This term is going to be a *riot!*"

He was familiar with the twins, having met them on the march to safety through Siberia what seemed like a lifetime ago. The three began talking about fighting techniques while the rest continued to demolish Chef Van's famous pancakes.

"BMW are off probation," Halli remarked with a smirk. "Kris from Charlie told me she's been assigned to them."

This was news to the Alpha kids, even Tina. "I didn't think they would be allowed to teach again. Bethany Anne —the Queen, I mean—was really pissed with them after...um."

Craig laughed loudly. "After they nearly blew up the moon—with you on it? Yeah, we *all* know about that."

A deep and reproachful voice boomed behind them. "*Do* you, Craig?"

The kids jumped—all except Tina. She wasn't afraid of her Uncle John.

John loomed above the table, muscles rippling as he folded his arms across his barrel of a chest. "Because *that* is classified information, and *you* shouldn't be spreading it. Damn Bobcat! I'll bet he's the one who told you," John continued, his brow furrowed menacingly.

Tina did her best not to giggle at the act, but couldn't contain herself.

John's frown deepened as concern washed over his face. "I'm serious, Tina. One snippet of information in the wrong hands could bring down everything we're trying to build out here. Do you want that? 'Loose lips sink ships.' Not good when your ship is in space."

"I'm sorry, John," Tina said, chastened. "I didn't mean to be disrespectful."

His face softened at her apology. "You weren't, Tina. Just remember that information is as good as hard currency out here and you'll be fine." John reassured her with a pat on the shoulder. "Now, where are my students?" Five kids raised their hands. "Follow me, then." John strode out of the cafeteria, followed by Maxim, Craig, Halli, and twin girls with whom Tina was unfamiliar.

"We should watch this," Yana said quietly. "Come, we will go to the bleachers. We have an hour before we have to be anywhere.

Academy Grounds, PET Annex

The newly-built physical education and training department, informally known as "the PET," had been commissioned by Bethany Anne to make the training program the Academy administrators had put in place possible. It was a state-of-the-art sports complex with all amenities, including a stadium which was accessed from the rear of the Academy. Tina wasn't one for unnecessary physical exertion beyond what it took to stay healthy and in shape, but she could appreciate the care that had gone into the creation of the new annex.

She was amused to see that her team were not alone in hoping to look in on her uncle's class. Most of the student body was making their way to the stadium—along with the resident staff. She waved to Diane and Dorene, the Academy administrators, as she passed them at the bottom of the steps to the entrance.

As always, Tina stopped to read the quote above the door. The quotes were one of her favorite things about the school's buildings.

"You dream. You plan. You reach. There will be obstacles. There will be doubters. There will be mistakes. But with hard work, with belief, with confidence and trust in yourself and those around you, there are no limits." The tiny script beneath showed the quote was from an Olympic swimming champion.

Good advice, she thought, hurrying to catch up with the others. She dashed to the spot in the front of the bleachers where they were just getting comfortable, which was within hearing distance of the dugout where John had settled in to wait for his students to join him after changing into their workout clothes. She waved at her uncle, who answered with a miniscule nod.

"I wonder if they'll be doing *real* fighting?" Ron speculated. "I mean, this is the advanced class. We go at it pretty hard in our regular training, and the obstacle course couldn't get any harder than it already is. What else could they be learning?"

"You just don't like to get physical, Ron. That's okay, but I would give my arm to be taking this class with Maxim. I bet they'll be fighting with weapons!" Nestor was practically drooling as he looked out across the stadium, imagining epic battles playing out on the sandy arena below.

John's class exited the changing rooms a moment later, clearly perturbed by the unexpected audience. They scanned the crowd, fidgeting and making last-minute adjustments to the new activewear they'd all been issued as they nervously approached the dugout where their mentor waited.

"Eyes on me, class." John didn't raise his voice...but then he never had to. The students obeyed instantly, lining up in front of John in silence.

He smiled at the five Wechselbalg kids to put them at ease. "Over the next six weeks I'll be teaching you some advanced combat techniques. We will also look at discipline, tactics and strategy, command structure, and begin your weapons training."

The class oohed and aahed as he ran through the list.

"This is just a taste of what awaits when you graduate," John continued. "You are the future of the Empire's security services. You may end up in the Guardians, or be more suited to another role. That might mean action, or something like diplomatic security—whatever the Empire requires of you." His tone became serious. "Wherever you go there will be people watching, so composure under scrutiny is vital to the job. The discipline to maintain that composure is your first line of defense against *any* attack."

Craig raised a hand, and John nodded to allow the boisterous Wechselbalg to speak. "Don't the Guardians just go in, kick ass, and haul out of there?" He turned to his classmates, and his face dropped when they just stared at him, horrified by his disrespectful question.

"Dude, this is exactly what he's talking about!" Halli hissed, hiding her face in her hand. "Just shut up and *listen*!"

John gave Craig the hairy eyeball. "Your friend is smart, Craig. Listen to her and you'll go far."

Craig had the decency to blush. "Sorry, sir."

John nodded. "I understand that military life looks like an action movie from the outside. There are times when the shock-and-awe approach is necessary, but that is not *all* we do. First and foremost, we are protectors. Reflect on why it's a bad idea to open your mouth without thinking while you're giving me fifty push-ups." He clapped his hands to get them moving. "All of you—come on, we haven't got all day!"

The kids glared at Craig as they hit the deck. The five Wechselbalg were fit and strong, and they pumped the push-ups out quickly. John nodded when they were all on their feet again. "Why do you think I made all of you do the push-ups?"

Maxim raised his hand. "Because a mistake by one is a mistake by all of us."

"Exactly. Each of your decisions leads to consequences for the other people on your team. Choose wisely. Maxim, you are team leader for today. Right, class. Warm up. How quickly do you think you can do this assault course?"

CHAPTER FOUR

Q BBS *Meredith Reynolds*, **Medical Wing**

Yana leant over Bai Hu, gently stroking the young boy's head to soothe his nightmare. She had come to look in on him on her way to her first day of shadowing Cheryl Lynn.

He was so small, definitely younger than Tina's brother, Todd. However old he was, he'd been through too much, she thought sadly.

He woke briefly, his eyes wide with fear until he saw it was Yana. He relaxed then, falling back into a fractured sleep while his nanocytes worked with the nutrients and medicines in his IV drip to heal him from his ordeal.

He had been this way since they came back from Mongolia. Bai Hu awoke for brief periods in terror, and only the sight of Yana or Peter Silvers could calm him. She had only just learned his name yesterday, as she had coaxed him to eat some of the clear broth Chef Van had made especially for him after she had told the chef the malnourished werecat wasn't keeping food down.

She kissed his forehead lightly and tucked him in again, then tiptoed out of his room. She was surprised to see the Queen approaching from the other end of the corridor with her dog, but she had no time to pet Ashur today. As she exited the Medical Wing she broke into a jog, anxious to be on time for her first day of class.

***

Yana arrived outside the large meeting room at the same time as a girl from Delta she vaguely recognized, and a boy she didn't know at all. The three looked at each other awkwardly for a moment. She realized that she didn't know either of them as well as she should; the bond she had forged with her team didn't leave much room for close friendships with the other kids. That would have to change.

She held out a hand. "I'm Yana, Alpha Class. Good to meet you both."

The boy took her hand with a smile. "Jayden and Ksenia. We're both from Delta."

The girl curtseyed. "I remember you from the journey. It is an honor to meet you, Your Highness."

Yana cut her off with a wave and an embarrassed smile. "Please, Ksenia, I'm just Yana. I want no part of being royalty. I swore my allegiance to the Queen just like you. Claiming titles you haven't earned is Earth-think, and we are beyond that now."

Ksenia nodded, still slightly starstruck.

Yana was relieved when Cheryl Lynn arrived, ending the exchange.

"Good morning class," she said, swiping the tablet she held. "Congratulations on showing an aptitude for leadership. I know I don't need to ask if you read through the packet I sent. Have you all met?"

They nodded, awed by the aura of competence their mentor radiated. "Good. I've just forwarded our schedule for the day to your tablets. Open them now, please."

Yana's eyes bulged when she saw the endless to-do list scrolling down the screen of her tablet. "Ms. Grimes?"

Cheryl Lynn smiled. "Yes, Yana?"

"How do you do all this in a day plus look after Tina and Todd...and still look this good?"

Her teacher's smile deepened. "That's the secret of good time management, Yana. It's one of the things we'll cover during the course of this term." She pointed at the tablet. "The first thing to learn is that your schedule is your friend. What's the first item on today's agenda? Oh, s... poop. We're going to be late. Quickly! We need to go inside and find seats." Her heels clicked impatiently on the hard floor as she ushered the three of them toward the door.

When they entered, the meeting room was filling up with people Yana had heard stories about but never met. Guardian Commander Silvers was deep in conversation with another Guardian in the front row, and she wondered how Bai Hu was doing. He was never far from her mind.

"What happened to good time management?" Jayden panted as they followed Cheryl Lynn on her power-climb to an empty row on the second tier.

Cheryl Lynn laughed merrily as she took a seat and waved to the students to do the same. "That's the second thing you need to know. Your schedule is your friend—

until it isn't. Make a plan, but be prepared to adapt if it goes sideways."

Ksenia spoke up. "What is this class, Ms. Grimes?"

Cheryl Lynn put her tablet on the desk in front of her and began rummaging around in her oversize bag. "Good question. This class is on Yollin culture."

"What does that have to do with what we're learning?" Jayden asked, head tilted to the side.

"Good question again!" Cheryl Lynn smiled, placing the pad and pen she'd pulled out of her bag on the desk beside the tablet. "I'm the one taking this class, Jayden. It's only for upper management—the people who will have direct contact with the Yollins at this time. You just get to sit in with me today. It's important to remember that you can't know everything, but you can do your best to keep learning and improving no matter what your age. It's doubly important for people who have responsibility for others on a large scale to keep a finger on the pulse of what's happening. If I don't keep up to date on develop- ments, it could be detrimental to the whole Empire." Her attention was drawn to the stage, where a Yollin stood at the lectern ready to begin talking. "*Shhh*, now. Class is starting."

CHAPTER FIVE

BBS *Meredith Reynolds,* Jean Dukes' R&D Labs

Q The escort deposited Tina and Ron in an office and told them to wait. They went to join the thin, pale boy at the refreshment stand behind the conference table.

Ron paused to take a closer look at the schematics pinned to the walls as he passed. "Hey, look at this," he marveled. "These must be the armor designs for Project Gauntlet. I heard my dad talking about it while I was on a call to my mom a couple of weeks ago."

The unfamiliar boy's shyness melted at the mention of armor. He approached and held a hand out in their direction. "I'm Aleksi Nikolayev, Bravo Class. What do you know about the new armor?"

Tina and Ron introduced themselves with a handshake. Ron was almost too happy to have an ear to bend about his latest obsession.

"It's a whole new way of looking at protection. The new

composites they're coming up with are going to change things." His eyes shone with glee at Aleksi's interest in the subject. "The Yollin scientist, Roylee, has shared her people's secrets with BMW, who are farming everything out to the appropriate departments. It's like a level-up for the plastics specialists. It's an exciting time to be a chemist!"

"Easy there, fanboy," Tina teased gently. "So the armor is made of Yollin plastic?"

Ron shook his head, his cheeks turning pink. "Not exactly. The techniques are Yollin, but for the moment we're still using Earth materials. The plastics are only one constituent, anyway. The rest is made up of various minerals from down on the mudball. There's a group of scientists in Europe who've developed a new isostatic pressing technique that makes the resulting composite almost indestructible. It's slow going right now, but my dad is working with Marcus to streamline the manufacturing process. When I asked him about it he said they were making armor for everyone, even for Wechselbalg when they change form—or at least that's the plan."

When Tina looked away from the schematics, the line between her eyes that appeared whenever she was thinking hard was there. Ron loved that line.

"How are the parts being made at the moment?" she asked.

Ron shrugged. "I have no idea. Factory robots, I suppose? Maybe partly automated, but they're more likely to be manned."

She opened her tablet with her stylus and started scribbling calculations. As the boys watched, the line between her eyes became more pronounced. A few minutes later she frowned again and turned her tablet around to show them her calculations.

"Look, this isn't sustainable. The Wechselbalg will need two, maybe three sets of armor, and after we go through the gate resources will not be readily available. The mudball governments are already doing their best to stop us from taking resources off-planet."

Ron looked nonplussed.

Aleksi was getting it. "That's not all," he said. "I've been gaming this, and there's going to come a point where there's a bottleneck in the growth of the Empire. That will be the true tipping point."

It was Tina's turn to be puzzled. "What do you mean?"

Aleksi opened his tablet and brought up a time-lapse simulation. It showed the *Meredith Reynolds* surrounded by a few tiny dots. "This is the fleet at the moment," he told them. "All of our ships, as far as I know. Watch what happens if I extrapolate the future outcome using the Empire's current growth rate as a baseline."

The tiny dots multiplied as the clock sped up and the *Meredith Reynolds* ventured deeper and deeper into space. They were joined by an array of larger dots, clearly ships.

"Empires expand," Aleksi said as the first planet appeared. "We have already made contact with the Yollins, so it is logical to surmise that contact with more species will follow as we venture into deep space. The new species will join the Empire in large numbers, because *nobody* makes friends like a human. They will join our business communities, live on our stations, and contribute to the economy—but most importantly, they will enlist in our military. Do you see where I am going with this?"

"Oh, I *do* see," Tina answered. "The military will be the biggest drain on our resources as it grows. Production for the military will have to be expanded to include new armor and weapons to accommodate the new species."

Ron chipped in, "Like the early empires of Earth. The Romans were a fine example of what you're both afraid will happen. They spread their armies, conquest to conquest, ever-expanding until it got too big to sustain itself and collapsed. What's the specific problem here?"

Tina scrolled to the appropriate equation. "It's a bottleneck. If the Empire grows too quickly, there will come a point where the availability of materials, the man-hours, or the capacity for production will be compromised to a point where it will endanger the Empire," Tina answered absentmindedly, having gone back to her calculations. "It's a shame 3-D printing hasn't developed well enough to be used for more than the basics. I mean, it's great that what they do now takes a load off engineering, but imagine if we could print calories. No more food substitutes!"

Ron ran with the idea. "The 'basics' aren't too shabby these days, Tina. 3-D printing has come a long way from where it was a few years ago. The future possibilities are astounding! What if we could print the armor with reliable circuitry embedded? That would solve the problem for Gauntlet, and production could be pushed ahead of schedule. Heck, it could even have nanotech running it. Imagine if we could create armor that shifts *with* the Wechselbalg?"

"I think we're a long way from that, Ron." Tina smiled.

"Is that what you want to do when you graduate? Armor tech?"

Ron shrugged. "I don't know…maybe. Hey, shall we go look for Jean? This is starting to feel like our first day with BMW."

They left the office and found her almost immediately. She held up a hand to tell them to wait while she finished the conversation she was having with a young woman in a white lab coat. They did their best not to be obvious in their eavesdropping, but Jean was paying no attention to them anyway.

"It's definitely not just been misplaced?"

The tech shook her head. "No, ma'am, it's been stolen. No trace of it in the systems whatsoever, and no trail to follow to find out who did it. I don't know how it could have happened! And it doesn't stop there. The facility is having recurring blackouts, and some of the equipment has been malfunctioning due to power surges. ADAM says the local power grid is fine. The problem is inside the castle somewhere."

Jean scowled. "Then you're going to have to go to the facility and move things along. We're on a tight schedule, and the Queen waits for no one. We need all that equipment disassembled and moved up here before it gets too dangerous to be down there."

The tech looked horrified. "But, ma'am, I can't go. Well, I could, but it would be pointless. Only you, Marcus, and Doctor Llewellyn understand the equipment well enough to get the breakdown back on schedule."

Jean swept an impatient hand toward the waiting students. "I have a class to teach, and I have this department to run. How do you suggest I do all that and visit Earth to play nanny to a bunch of scientists as well?"

The tech shrugged. "You could always take the kids with you. They're pretty smart. They could help and learn on the job. Practical experience will do them good."

Jean looked at them again. They shuffled awkwardly, trying not to show the excitement they felt at the thought of visiting a genuine European castle.

"I'll get back to you tomorrow with my decision."

The tech nodded and hurried off. Jean waved the kids over and fixed them with a bright smile.

"Although I was supposed to come get *you*, welcome to my world. Looks like we're all going to Wales."

QBBS *Meredith Reynolds*, Jean's and John's Quarters, Later that Evening

"Oh…that's good. A little higher? There, that's the spot!" Jean groaned with pleasure as John used his considerable strength to destroy the stubborn knot in her upper back. "I swear, there are not enough hours in the day."

"Tough day at work, babe?" John asked, kissing Jean's head gently and pressing his cheek to hers for a brief moment. He could feel her weariness. She was working like a demon, as always.

Life was never dull around Jean. She was a firework contained in the body of an angel. Her inner and outer strength had drawn him to her. Her fiery spirit outshone even Bethany Anne's in his eyes, and her strength was a beacon that called him home to her whenever the darkness threatened to descend. It was his honor to be hers in return, and his good fortune to have realized it.

She followed him to the kitchen, where he snagged two glasses and a bottle of something darkly amber and steered her to the sofa in the lounge. Jean lay back with a sigh, removed her socks, and accepted the glass from him.

"Tell me all about it," John soothed.

She groaned again as he rubbed her tired feet and let her head fall onto the pillow behind her after taking a sip of her drink. "It's not the kids. The kids are great! Ronnie Diamantz especially—that kid can think outside the box! If I don't snag him when he graduates, I'm going on the warpath."

"He's got a lot of potential," John agreed. Jean lifted her head to look at him quizzically.

"He's friends with Tina," he clarified.

"She's my other star, but I know she's going to end up in R&D. Hey, remember that show—the guy who got in a ridiculous situation every week and got out of it using gum wrappers and cuckoo spit, or something?"

"*MacGyver?*"

Jean grinned. "That's the one. That's Tina. You have a problem, she has a solution."

That was high praise from Jean. John put a little more effort into the foot rub. "I don't understand half the stuff they say to each other."

"I do, and I'm beyond impressed by all three of them." Jean grimaced. "That's my issue. I'm still having problems at the Conwy facility, and I'm concerned they're not getting enough of my time. They deserve my full attention."

"What's the problem with the facility?" He hadn't been down there at all. The acquisition and security checks for that facility had gone through Nathan.

"That's what I need to get to the bottom of. There's something fishy going on there, and it's going to put Project Gauntlet behind if I don't address it." She reached over and grabbed her tablet from the table, passing it to John after a few swipes.

He looked through the documents, seeing the places where Jean had highlighted discrepancies in the facility's inventory records. "Looks like someone is stealing. Easy enough to remedy."

"Not just that." She swiped again, and there was highlighted computer code on the screen. "See this? This code doesn't belong in the facility's computers. They've been hacked."

John was instantly concerned. "How were they hacked? Didn't ADAM see it happening?"

"It was ADAM who brought it to my attention. He said he fixed the hacking problem, but I need to go down there in person to deal with the malfunctioning equipment. *Gott Verdammt!* I can't delegate this one—it's too sensitive. I'm going to have to take my techs down there to take over the disassembly while I take Laura off to repair the broken machinery, and what about the kids?"

Her misery was absolute, and tugged at John's natural urge to protect his lover from any and all pain. He scooted up to wrap an arm around her, his brow furrowed as he searched for a solution to her problem. "I wish I could help, babe."

Jean's distress slowly resolved into a subtle smile as she

leaned into his shoulder. "One of my team suggested I take them down with me...but I can't see a way around the security issues."

John erupted in snorting laughter. "*HA!* You've got the smarter half of Alpha Class, so they're going to need more than one adult to supervise them—especially after Mongolia. They get into trouble every time they go down there! I wouldn't let them out with anything less than a full security team." John became aware that he had walked right into her trap the moment the words left his mouth.

"Oh, *honey*! How sweet of you to volunteer!" She actually batted her eyelashes at him. How was he supposed to get out of this now?

"Babe, I'd love to help out but I have my regular duties and a class of my own to teach. If I could, I'd go just to protect Tina, since trouble follows her like a magnet. Thing is, even if I thought it was a good idea, Bethany Anne would never go for it."

Jean smiled knowingly. "Let's ask her, shall we? Meredith, would you ask the Queen if she has a moment to speak with us, please?"

"Certainly, Jean." Meredith's cool voice came from somewhere above them.

Bethany Anne's voice replaced the EI's a moment later, though it came from behind them when she appeared in the corner of the room kept clear for that purpose. "If it isn't everybody's favorite power couple! What can I do for you both?" She slid onto the sofa next to John and put her booted feet on the footrest, adjusting the legs of her deep purple slacks so they didn't wrinkle.

John grinned roguishly. "Looking good, boss. One might say you look as good as a well-manicured—"

"Before the words 'trophy wife' leave your mouth, remember I didn't have time for training yesterday," Bethany Anne purred dangerously. "I've got some frustration to work off, and I might decide that you're the only sparring partner I need tonight." Her expression became one of pure delight as the color drained from John's face.

Jean cut in before John could dig himself in farther. "I have an issue at the Conwy site that requires my personal attention. I want to take my class with me but two of them are Alpha and we all know they're a security risk. John doesn't think you'll let him off the leash long enough to accompany us to Earth." She fetched a glass for Bethany Anne and poured her a drink while John made excuses about not going down to Earth.

"Conwy…isn't that the castle I bought for Laura Llewellyn's outfit?"

Jean nodded. "The same. There's something off. Machinery breaking down, stolen data, missing inventory. It smells of sabotage to me."

Bethany Anne screwed up her nose. "Isn't the UK government playing nice anymore?"

Jean shrugged. "You can never tell with the British. They smile to your face, but you can tell they're lying through their teeth the whole time. They're just waiting for an opportunity to get their hands on our tech. There haven't been any overt attacks against us yet—that I know of, anyway."

Bethany Anne's eyes glazed over momentarily. "ADAM says they've stepped up surveillance, but you're right. And it might be the last chance the kids get to see Earth before it gets too dangerous. John, you can go."

"I have a class," he protested. "Duties!"

Jean snorted. "He just doesn't want to go down to the mudball with Alpha Class."

"Not true," he argued. "It's Craig I don't want to take down there. I intend to see him through to the end of the year with both hands intact. That boy has no inhibitions at all, but he's got a heart of gold. I keep watching and waiting for him to push it too far again."

"How come he was assigned to you if he's such a goof?" Bethany Anne asked.

"He needs it. Don't get me wrong—the General made a great start on straightening him out when he had him, but he's going to be an adult soon. If he doesn't start showing some maturity then he's not gonna make the cut for the Guardians." He ran a hand over his head and sighed. "He has the potential to be one of the best one day, Peter says the same. All we have to do is keep him alive long enough to reach it. He's all action, with no thought behind it. I miss having Peter to straighten out, I wish they were *all* as easy to slap the stupid out of as he was."

Bethany Anne laughed, smacking her leg. "Is that so? Maybe Craig needs something like a trip to Earth to help him shape up and take things seriously. You know as well as I do, those kids are our best and brightest—our future. Let them learn to protect each other."

She swirled the amber liquid around her glass and drank it in one gulp. "I wish I could still enjoy this. Okay, this is what you're going to do: your class is reassigned to Jean's class until further notice, and they will provide close protection—under your guidance, of course. Will that suffice, Jean?"

Jean nodded, one corner of her mouth turning up slightly.

John sighed. He knew when he was defeated. "Your wish is my command, my Queen."

"Good to hear," Bethany Anne replied with a smirk. She was about to say something else when she went blank again for a moment. "Gotta go. Ashur is having an issue."

John turned his sternest gaze on Jean after the Queen vanished.

"So, lover, when did you decide I was coming with you?"

The corner of her mouth was still upturned. "This afternoon, dear."

QBBS *Meredith Reynolds*, Bethany Anne's Suite

She strode out of her closet and assessed the situation. The lead-lined box Marcus had made for the Sacred Clan boy's necklace lay open on the floor, the mystery pendant in a puddle of chain-links beside it.

The chair was upturned and the pillows from the bed were scattered around the room. Ashur crouched in attack mode on the bed, barking furiously at the necklace.

She was by his side in less than a second, stroking the thick fur of his neck to calm him. She spoke softly but firmly. "Ashur, sit your ass down! What are you acting up for?"

Ashur laid down on the bed, but his hackles remained up and he directed a low snarl at the open box on the floor.

"What the hell is wrong with you?" she asked softly. "It's not active."

Ashur whined piteously. Bethany Anne wrapped her arms around him, gently placing her chin on his head. "What do you mean it's hurting your ears? TOM, is the necklace doing something to Ashur?"

The pendant is emitting a high-frequency signal. That would explain Ashur's discomfort.

She sat up and listened hard. "I can't hear anything, TOM."

Canine hearing is much more sensitive than human hearing. Even though yours is exceptional, his is even better. Ashur's enhancement must be making it unbearable for him.

Ashur chuffed sadly in confirmation of TOM's theory.

Bethany Anne put the necklace inside the box and snapped the lid shut, and Ashur instantly relaxed. She began to massage the dog's neck and shoulders, bringing a sigh of contentment from him as he lay down, his panic over.

"Interesting. The lead is blocking the signal completely. Sorry about that, Ashur. TOM, have you figured out what the necklace does yet? Or how the Sacred Clan ended up with technology from the Five?"

Not yet, but I'm sure I recognize it from somewhere. ADAM and I were able to trace it back to the time of Genghis Khan's reign, but the trail went cold after that. We pinpointed the location of our werecat's home using the Chinese military reports, but it's not good news. From what we can gather, there were no survivors in the boy's village.

Her heart broke for Bai Hu. She'd visited him with Ashur earlier, intending to check he wasn't a Sacred Clan plant. Her search of the sleeping werecat's mind had brought tears to her eyes, and she'd had to have TOM dial her emotions down before they overwhelmed her. "That poor kid. He'll have to stay with us, then. Nicholas Konstantinov has offered to take him in. His daughter was there when he was found, and they've bonded. What about this signal? What is its purpose?"

I don't know, but it calls to me. I can only surmise that it attracts attention.

Quit beating about the bush or that cozy bedroom will be a distant memory. What kind of attention?

Her mental teasing aside, Bethany Anne could feel TOM's discomfort as he spoke. **The Kurtherian kind. I don't think it's safe to have it up here, Bethany Anne.**

The whole point is to keep the Kurtherians away from Earth. If it's going to attract them, it needs to be hidden for humanity's safety. How about hiding it back on Earth? It's been safe enough down there up until now.

I don't think it will be anymore. Every flight to Earth is being monitored, and then there is the added risk of it falling into Majestic's hands.

True. The last thing we need is those lunatics getting hold of Kurtherian tech. Even if they don't, eventually someone will find it and open it. We don't want that. She continued to massage Ashur, letting the rhythm be her focus as she turned the problem over in her mind. "I have a solution," she said aloud as she picked the box up and strode purposefully toward her closet. "Come on, Ashur, let's go for a little trip."

Where are we going?

"To the *Archangel*, I'm going to hide it there for now. I'll figure it out once we get through that damned Gate."

Ashur pressed his head against her side and wagged his tail, eager to get going. She placed a hand on his back and vanished.

CHAPTER SIX

Q BBS *Meredith Reynolds*, Stores

The mood on the tram was light, the carefree camaraderie between the students reminded Jean of the early days of her military career. These were the brightest of the academic kids, and the most proficient of the physically-oriented ones. Some of the kids met both criteria, thanks to the training Diane and Dorene had integrated into the curriculum. She thought they were growing into fine young adults.

Jean addressed the students as the tram pulled to a stop outside the entrance to the docking bays. "Get in there and requisition the items on your checklist from Isaac, then reconvene here as soon as you're done to catch the tram back to the Academy. Make sure you all get a good night's sleep! We leave first thing tomorrow, so make sure you don't forget anything—because it will be too late."

Halli nudged Craig in the ribs and gleefully whispered, "She means you!"

"I mean *all* of you, Halli," Jean admonished the girl.

"Going down to Earth—even to a friendly nation—is dangerous. Our allies would not hesitate to turn against us if they were presented with an opportunity to gain the upper hand. Failing to prepare is preparing to fail—remember that. There's no room for half-assed efforts when the stakes are this high. Now go."

The kids grabbed their bags and poured out of the door as soon as it opened, spilling onto the platform and flocking as one to the Stores' entrance. Jean grinned, buoyed by the students' inexhaustible energy, and went to catch up with John.

Tina and Ron were delighted to be reunited with Maxim so soon. Tina had that pre-vacation feeling, and she was not the only one.

"Whoooo! Goin' to the mudball!" Craig sing-songed as he ran in a circle doing a series of handsprings. The contents of his pockets left a trail behind him. He completed his circle and slipped on the penlight he'd dropped, landing flat on his back with a resounding *oomph.*

The twins rolled their eyes and sniggered. "I swear, Masha," Mischa purred. "It's like having an infant on the team!"

Halli shot icy daggers at them from her eyes, which took on a yellow gleam. "If either of you say another word…" She pointed two fingers at her eyes, then at Masha and Mischa in turn before going to help Craig up.

"Ignore those two. They're upset because they don't want to leave the *Meredith Reynolds*," Aleksi said quietly to Halli as she passed him.

"Enough of this. We should get inside and find Isaac,"

Maxim said, taking charge. Craig finished picking his things up from the floor and they all went into Stores.

Isaac was waiting for them when, armed with their checklists, they arrived at the requisitions desk.

"You got cleared to go down there again?" Isaac didn't try to hide his surprise when Maxim handed his checklist over first. "Oh, it's just the UK. Wales, hey? You're lucky—they love us there for putting so much into the economy. You'll be fine. We're buying a lot from them at the moment. It's one of the few places that still does business with us openly."

He finished transferring the requests to his EI Mischale, and grabbed his jacket. "Follow me."

QBBS *Meredith Reynolds*, Cafeteria

The next morning the cafeteria was bustling with students and staff alike, all in search of breakfast. Tina took her tray over to the unofficial Alpha Class table and sat down on the bench next to Yana.

"So how is class with my mother?" she asked, peeling her banana.

Yana's eyes lit up. "It is everything I hoped. You are so lucky to have a mother like her! Did you enjoy your dinner together last night? She was anticipating it all day."

Tina grinned as she opened her yogurt and sliced the banana into the cup. "We had a great time, thanks. How about you, did you have a good visit with your dad?"

Yana shook her head. "I did not go home. I stayed with Bai Hu instead, and Papa brought dinner to the medical wing. We had Chinese food. It was delicious, but we all ate too much, even Bai Hu!"

"How is he?" Tina was impressed with Yana's dedication to the kid they'd rescued. He had been near death when they'd found him hiding from the Chinese army in a ruin in Mongolia, and Yana had made time every day to visit despite her full schedule.

Yana's face brightened considerably. "He is almost well enough to leave Medical. Papa has arranged for him to stay in our home. I always wanted a little brother!"

Tina was happy for her friend. "Just wait until he starts *acting* like a little brother. You'll look back on this moment and kick yourself for your naiveté!" Maxim and Nestor joined in her amusement.

"It is always good to have a brother, even if he helps himself to your breakfast!" Nestor pulled his tray away from Maxim and stuffed the remainder of his bacon into his mouth. "So, you are going to the mudball without me. Try not to get shot at this time."

"I will do my best," Maxim replied fondly. "As *you* will be careful not to crash any fighters into our home!" He threw an arm around Nestor's neck and applied his knuckles in the age-old expression of brotherly love.

Nestor squirmed unsuccessfully to get out of the noogie, but his cousin let him go a second later.

Maxim continued, "I have to say, I *am* concerned about going back down to the mudball."

"Why's that, now?" Craig asked, getting up from the Bravo Class table and sitting with them. "You heard Isaac. It's going to be 'a jolly old time, chap.' They love TQB in Wales."

Ron groaned at Craig's terrible attempt at a British accent. "Dude, take it from me...*don't* do that while we're down there, okay?"

Maxim reddened, not seeing the funny side of Craig's shenanigans. "I do not understand why you think this is funny," he rebuked the other boy. "You do not take anything seriously. We have seen firsthand the dangers of returning to Earth, and they are not to be taken lightly. You are the oldest student in this school, but you act like a little kid. Grow up before you cost someone their life!"

Yana backed Maxim up. "Maxim is right. We had not one, but *two* armies firing on us, and not just guns. They fired missiles at us, Craig!"

Craig looked around the table for support, but saw only agreement in everyone's face. His cheer melted away. "If it was that bad we wouldn't be allowed to go. The UK is our ally."

Tina nodded. "Did you hear a word of what Ms. Dukes said? They are only our allies because they want our technology, Craig. Every single government on Earth is looking out for itself instead of the future of the human race. Everyone who's on our side is up here in space already, or is preparing to move up to the *Meredith Reynolds*."

Craig looked thoughtful for a moment, then his usual grin reappeared on his face. "You all worry too much. It's a vacation in a freaking *castle*, for crying out loud!"

He got up and took his tray to the wash pile. They watched him go with concerned expressions all around.

Yana was first to speak. "Please be careful down there, even if he won't be."

"I do not think he will have a choice, Yana. Our class is providing security for Ms. Dukes' team. John Grimes will accept nothing but our complete focus and dedication to the job."

Yana was staring off into the distance again. She always wore that look when she daydreamed about John.

"Earth to Yana," Tina said, waving a hand in front of her friend's face.

"Huh?" Yana snapped back to reality.

"Your tablet is bleeping." Tina pointed at the tablet.

Yana gasped. "My schedule!" She slung her bag over her shoulder and grabbed her tablet in one hand and her breakfast muffin in the other, and made a run for it. "Have fun storming the castle!"

"We will," they answered, and she was gone.

CHAPTER SEVEN

U K Airspace, Bethany Anne's Pod
The Queen's Pod swept toward the emerald-green islands below. In front of it were the two passenger Pods carrying Jean and John's teams, and to the rear were the two Black Eagles flown by Guardians assigned to John. The Pod had been given more upgrades since their trip to the Great Wall, now it boasted even more weapons—and a cloaking device. Bethany Anne wanted to make sure that the kids weren't left vulnerable again after the disaster in Mongolia.

They had been joined by four fighter jets provided by the RAF to 'keep them safe from attackers.' The jets had been waiting for them when they'd entered British airspace.

"It was nice of them to send an escort," Masha said, looking out of the window at the two jets stationed on each side of the small convoy.

John chuckled. "They're not exactly friendly, Masha. It's in the RAF's interest to know where we are."

Ron was practically drooling, his face and hands pressed against the Pod's window so he could see more clearly. "Those are Eurofighter Typhoons! They're so good as a multirole fighter they're used all over the world. The RAF haven't found anything better to replace them, and I know for a fact that they tried."

"They're not very aerodynamic—at least compared to our Black Eagles," Mischa remarked, pointing at the two Black Eagles flanking the second passenger Pod carrying the rest of John and Jean's personnel. "See how sleek *they* are?"

"All I want to know is how long until we get there?" Aleksi was even paler than usual. "I don't feel so good."

"You're looking pretty green around the gills there, buddy." John's voice was soothing as he tucked Aleksi under one gigantic arm and guided him back to his seat. "Get yourself strapped in, kid. We'll be there soon."

He passed Aleksi a paper bag and a bottle of water. "Do you suffer from motion sickness?"

"No, sir," Aleksi replied, trying to get the cap off the bottle with shaky fingers.

John held his hand out for the bottle, twisting the cap off with ease. "Are you sick?"

Aleksi shook his head. "No, I'm afraid of flying, sir."

John placed a hand on Aleksi's shoulder. "It's okay, Aleksi. Everybody feels afraid sometimes. Even *I'm* afraid sometimes." He nodded, confirming that he wasn't pulling their legs.

"Not *you*, surely?" Maxim was incredulous. This man was his hero; one of the men he modeled his own growing sense of masculinity upon in his father's absence. He had been at the Queen's side from the very beginning. How could a man such as this fear *anything*?

John nodded stoically. "Even me. Seeing as it's the anniversary soon, let me tell you about the time I almost died in a swamp in Florida, back when I was a regular human."

Jean pulled her headset down and looked at him from where she sat in front of the control panel. "You'd better keep it PG-13, John. Remember your audience."

"Of course, honey!" He winked at the kids as he said it, grinning as soon as Jean's back was turned and her headset was back in place. "It was like this: Back then we knew nothing about nanocytes or aliens. When we met Bethany Anne for the first time we believed she was a vampire, and a *very scary* one, to boot. We picked her up from the airport that day, and every one of us felt our approaching deaths when her plane landed."

"Did she try to suck your blood?" Everyone groaned at Craig's question.

"Grow up!" Mischa sneered. "The Queen does not suck people's blood!"

"She does too!" Craig argued. "I've seen the video of her doing it!"

John ignored the bickering, his expression wistful as he revisited the memory of the day his life had changed forever. "She didn't suck our blood. She made us *laugh*! We listened to her in the SUV on the way back to the base after picking her up, trying not to crap ourselves. She came out with the crudest things! We laughed so hard and so long we almost crashed! The boss—Dan Bosse, to be exact — thought she'd killed us all and started panicking."

He laughed loudly. "That's the secret to banishing fear —there's a funny side to almost any situation, and if you can find it you can get through anything."

"So how did you almost die?" Aleksi asked.

John's face grew serious. "That came later. We were sent on our first mission as a team— four awesome humans and a brand-new vampire none of us knew for sure we could trust. We located the Nosferatu hiding in the swamp, but then we found out there were more headed for the base. The Queen left the four of us—that's me, Scott, Eric, and Darryl—to take care of the Nosferatu in the swamp while she went back and saved everyone in camp from the group of the ba...asshats who were coming for them."

"Language, John," Jean called over her shoulder.

"I'm doing my best, Jean. *Shh*, you're spoiling the story!"

All the students including Tina stared up at him wide-eyed, waiting for him to continue. She had heard this story before many times, but she loved hearing it straight from her uncle's mouth.

"So what happened next, sir?" Maxim asked breathlessly.

John made a show of looking around. "What happened next was, we fought the Nosferatu. It toyed with us. Remember we weren't enhanced. My arm was broken, and I'd been stabbed in the chest. I was bleeding out with no hope of getting medical attention. I knew that was it for me. *Gott Verdammt*, I was sh—"

Jean coughed pointedly.

"*Sure*, Jean. I was going to say 'sure,' that it was the end for me." He waved her off. "In that moment, I was more afraid than I had ever been in my life. More than all the times I went into battle against the monsters combined. I didn't want to die in the middle of a stinking swamp in the 'Glades at the hands of a Nosferatu. As I lay there bleeding, I realized something." He paused, the tension filling the seating area as the students hung on his every word.

"What?" Maxim breathed.

He leaned forward. "That it didn't matter so much that I was going to die. It mattered that I would die fighting for what's *right*. Protecting others. *That* was what made the fear go away."

"That, and a pick-me-up from Bethany Anne!" Jean joked from the control panel. "Get yourselves ready for landing, kids. We'll be wheels-down in ten."

"Wheels-down?" Masha asked.

"Ten *what?*" Mischa added, having been paying more attention to John's story than Jean's announcement.

"We're landing in ten minutes," Tina told the puzzled Wechselbalg twins.

United Kingdom, North Wales, Conwy

Tina was enthralled by the view as the Pod swept along the coast. She saw wild seas thrashing the cliffs as birds swooped and dived along the waves. Pretty beaches led into picturesque towns, and then to rolling farmland dotted with sheep. On the horizon were hills and mountains in every shade of green and gray.

The Pod slowed and changed course slightly, heading inland over a river as they made their final approach to the castle. The RAF fighters peeled away with a roaring *swoosh* when the castle walls came into sight, escort duty done.

Jean maneuvered the Pod so she could land in the open courtyard of the castle. She cut the engines and checked that it was safe to exit, dropping the ramp halfway when the EI confirmed that it was.

The passenger Pods landed next, followed by the Black Eagles.

"Who's meeting us?" John asked Jean.

Jean looked up from the console. "Doctor Laura Llewellyn and her team. Bethany Anne bought the castle and had them moved up here when her first setup was compromised. I'm hoping that the equipment issues are just malfunctions and not sabotage. Either way, you kids keep eyes on each other the whole time we're down there." She focused on Tina, Ron, and Aleksi. "You three will be assisting me throughout our time here. If you know something, or you get an idea you think will help expedite the breakdown of the facility, speak up. Our priority is to get everything up to the *Meredith Reynolds*. Do *not* wander off or go exploring without supervision. And *no* poking around, got it?" The kids nodded. "Good. This is a working chemical plant, among other things, and you all have a reputation for being in the place the explosions are going off. There will be none of that while I'm responsible for you all."

"That goes double for my class," John said sternly. "You stick to your assigned student no matter what, just like we practiced doing in class. You got me? I will be watching, as will my team, but we cannot be everywhere at once—especially if there's a saboteur at work. Keep each other safe."

"You'd think a castle would be harder to infiltrate," Jean grumbled.

"Not necessarily, Ms. Dukes," Ron piped up. "A lot of these castles had secret passages built in so the occupants could escape in an emergency. If you had a map, you could get in and out with no problems—unless the tunnel had collapsed, I suppose."

"There will be no exploring of abandoned tunnels, Ronald Diamantz." Jean's tone made it clear there would be no further discussion on the matter. She gestured toward the ramp. "Out you go."

"I'm first. Wait until I've made sure it's safe out there." John left the Pod and swept the area with his expert eye, giving the students the same level of protection he gave Bethany Anne.

He waved them out when he was finished, satisfied the open courtyard was secure. "It doesn't matter if the EI tells you it's safe," he told his students. "As the person in charge of security, you still go first and see for yourself. You are responsible."

A small plump woman wearing a disheveled lab coat came out of the heavily barred doors and hurried toward them.

She looked longingly at the array of Pods in the courtyard. "Bloody Hell, it's like Camelot meets *Star Journey*. TQB?" She squinted up into John's face as she put her glasses on. Her squint was replaced by a frown when she saw him clearly. "You're not who I was expecting. Where's Jean?"

"Hello, Laura," Jean interjected, holding a hand out to the woman. "Nice to finally meet you in person. This is

John, my personal security. I also brought three of my brightest and best to lend a hand."

Tina and the others waved from the top of the ramp. Panic flashed over her face for a brief second. "Kids? This isn't really the place for kids, Jean. They could get hurt."

Jean smiled knowingly. "They're not ordinary kids, Laura. They're the cream of the crop, and my 'future replacements,' if I may quote the Academy administrators directly. You'll be glad of their input before we're done— you'll see." She steered the doctor toward the castle door.

Tina was warmed to her core by the praise from Jean. She knew her future lay in science, and all science came down to engineering in the end. She grabbed her bag and followed the adults into the imposing castle.

Doctor Llewellyn was still talking to Jean when Tina entered the refurbished interior. John escorted the students up a spiraling stone staircase, which opened onto an oddly familiar-looking hallway.

Tina walked slowly around the circular hallway, touching the thick tapestries that were interspaced with elaborate wall sconces along the walls. She took in the painstaking detail on the rug that graced the smooth stone floor, which depicted a mountain scene. She looked at the three doors leading off from the windowless hall. The space where the fourth would have been was taken up by a carved stone fireplace. It was the details that caught her eye—the colors of the fabrics, and the items atop of the chunky mantelpiece.

John caught her attention and pointed to the closest door. "This way, Teeny."

"Ugh, don't call me that!" She laughed and stuck her

tongue out as she flounced past him into the dorm room. Her suspicions were confirmed when she saw the comfortable living arrangements within. There was a seating area, a kitchenette, and a door to what Tina presumed was a bathroom, as well as five bunk beds in a partitioned area at the back of the room, with soft bedding folded neatly on the end of each one.

She turned to John, who still stood in the doorway. "Bethany Anne had this made, didn't she? I recognize the color scheme we used to have at the Colorado base."

John nodded. "It had to be almost completely refurbished. This place was almost a ruin when Bethany Anne bought it and had it repurposed for Doctor Llewellyn's work."

"I love how stylish it all is," Halli said, ruffling the crushed velvet curtains as she entered the dormitory. "It's like medieval times without all the stink!"

John laughed at that. "I'm going to leave you kids to get settled in. I'll be in the suite next door if you need me for anything. Remember, no wandering around! I'll be back to get you in an hour for dinner."

United Kingdom, North Wales, Undisclosed Location

"Well, man? Did they take the bait? Spit it out, now."

Broadbent winced at the sharpness of the voice coming through the telephone speaker. He swallowed and adjusted the old Bakelite handset against his ear.

"It appears so, sir, but not in the way we had hoped. The Dukes woman has been drawn in by the sabotage as planned, but she has brought that muscle-bound brute, John Grimes, with her."

"Which one is that, now?" the voice demanded.

Broadbent sighed. He'd already given the higher-ups a full brief on every known member of TQB Enterprises. Not that they'd bothered reading it. "John Grimes, sir. The head of security himself. Look, sir. May I speak freely for a moment?"

Silence on the line. Then a short grunt which Broadbent took as assent.

"Sir, if we go up against him, we die. If he doesn't kill us all, then *She* will. I know they have been an absolute pain in the rear when it comes to Wales, but intelligence is telling us they are preparing to leave."

The voice was cold. "That is why you are going to get that armor for us, Broadbent. If they leave and we get nothing from it then why have we been so accommodating? We are being hounded out of the UN for our continued relationship with TQB. If they will not share their advantages it is up to *us* to take them for ourselves!"

"And by us, you mean me."

The voice sounded surprised that Broadbent was even asking. "Of course I do, you imbecile. Otherwise what's the point of keeping you around? Black-ops aren't cheap to run, you know. Now go and get me the Project Gauntlet armor, *whatever it takes*. The weaponry alone will put us light years ahead of anyone else, do not stop until you secure it!"

The line went dead and Broadbent replaced the receiver in its cradle. His orders weighed heavily on him. He was from the local area originally, which was why he had been assigned to 'the Conwy farce' – as he'd been privately calling this mission for weeks.

He had joined MI5 as a fresh-faced university graduate with the naïve assumption that he would boldly save the nation from all that sought to cause harm. Twenty years later his outlook had changed. Now, he just sucked up whatever they threw at him and got on with things as best as he could. One shady mission after another had left his shining armor tarnished, to say the least.

Kidnapping innocent British citizens, that was a new low. Involving children always made him feel sick to his stomach but that was the way his duty went sometimes.

He sighed as he left the office, making sure the door was locked behind him before heading for the briefing room.

CHAPTER EIGHT

United Kingdom, North Wales, Conwy Castle, Labs
The underground manufacturing floor thrummed loudly with the noise of the workers shutting down the production line. Ron's guess had been mostly correct—the production was handled by robots, but the robots were fully controlled by humans.

Tina stood with Ron, and Aleksi at a workbench near the machine Jean was working on, taking notes. Jean had clipped a tiny camera to her lapel and set it to send a live feed to the students' tablets so they could get a close-up of the problem.

"Hey," Aleksi called to Halli as she walked by, but she didn't make eye contact or reply—just skimmed her gaze over them as she took in the details of the room on her way through.

"It's weird that they won't talk to us," he complained. Even Craig had abandoned his joker act, doing nothing to distract Jean or her class from their work.

Tina, who was used to bodyguards, reassured him. "If they're chatting, their focus isn't on their job."

"I still find it strange," was all Aleksi had to say.

"Pass me the Allen keys, one of you," Jean shouted from under the chassis of the huge assembly robot. "*Gott Verdammt* British engineering. Who decided that *this* was a better system than a simple wrench?"

Tina grabbed the bunch of hex keys from the tool cart beside the workbench and slid them along the floor toward her teacher. "Is the whole compartment bolted down with them, Ms. Dukes?"

"You know, the Allen key was invented by an American," Ron whispered conspiratorially behind his hand to Tina, who just shook her head slowly at him.

A muffled curse came from underneath the chassis. Jean slid out a moment later, covered in dust and cobwebs. "You do know that I can still hear you when you whisper, Mr. Diamantz."

Ron blushed at being called out.

Jean was too preoccupied with the tool cart to chastise him any further. "And yes, Tina. Worse, not one of those keys fits, so I'm going to take my trusty hammer and persuade them that it's in their best interest to cooperate." She slid back underneath the silent machine and removed the problem the old-fashioned way. "Elbow grease," she called between the clangs. "And engineering."

Aleksi spoke up. "If you don't have what you need, change what you have to fit the purpose."

"Exactly, Aleksi." Jean praised the boy from underneath the machine. "And if *that* doesn't work, hit it really hard a few times. The screen wobbled as she hit the protruding bolts one at a time with the claw end of her hammer. Each blow landed precisely, shearing the heads of the bolts clean off. "That is an excellent use of my enhanced strength," she chuckled.

The view on the screen steadied as Jean eased the panel off. There was a rattle and another clang as the access panel finally came free in her hand. "What the... This is worse than I thought. Zoom in on your screens and tell me what you see, kids."

"Oh, geez," Ron said in a pained voice. "Looks like someone rigged a foam canister to go off in there."

Tina zoomed in on the bright orange hard-as-concrete expanding foam almost completely covering the inside of the compartment. "It's a mess!"

Jean concurred. "It's going to take me a while to get this operational again. Lucky for you this is not class with BMW. I got with the program and prepared a little some-thing for you to do if there was a day like this. Open your tablet menu and select the app named 'Bootstrapping.' You may as well have some fun while I'm busy."

Tina opened the app and began exploring the menu. "This is cool!"

"What's this for, Ms. Dukes?" Ron asked. "It looks like a game."

"It *is* a game!" Aleksi cheered.

"It's not a game, Aleksi," Jean corrected him. "Well, it's not *just* a game. It's a battle simulation. The aim is to work as a team to manage your resources and defend your base against attack. I'll be done in a couple of hours or so."

"*Cool!*" Ron skipped through the available scenarios.

"Looks like we can change the difficulty level, and the location, too. No way! It's the *Meredith Reynolds*!"

Tina glanced up from reading the instructions. "That's a challenging one. The scenarios are all *'Star Journey'* or *'Galaxy Battles'* fanfics made up by BMW. We should choose one of the Earth locations for our first try. They're all based on historical events, sort of."

"What about this one?" Ron showed them another scenario. "I know a lot about Gettysburg."

Aleksi typed furiously. "One minute. I have something else that I think you'll both like." He sent them each an attachment to download. "I just need to load the plans and inventory for this facility into the game. What do you think?"

Tina opened the castle layout on her tablet. "I like the idea, but there's no defense tech here. What are we supposed to defend it with?"

They all heard Jean laugh. "That's why it's called 'Bootstrapping'. You have to build your defenses using the facility's inventory. Good job, Aleksi! You kids enjoy yourselves, now."

They had already turned their attention to the game.

Maxim shook his head fondly as he passed them on his patrol a while later. He admired the way the three of them could completely absorb themselves in a problem. Nestor was the same—the same dreamy expression passed over his cousin's face whenever an idea popped into his head. Maxim admired their ability to lose themselves, even if he didn't want to be that way himself. He could never allow himself to be so unaware of his surroundings.

Today's lesson in forward planning and preparation trickled through his mind as he walked the stone corridors, his steps echoing softly from the high walls. The castle's refurbishment team hadn't managed to extend the cheery atmosphere to the connecting corridors between the labs in the lower levels of the castle. Despite the plush carpets and wall tapestries, the cold sea wind still leached through the outer walls. He heard a hushed voice from up ahead that he would have missed without his enhanced hearing. It was Doctor Llewellyn, and she sounded distressed. He hurried on silent feet to the door he heard her voice coming from, which was ajar. He listened for a moment to make sure he wasn't disturbing a private disagreement.

Doctor Llewellyn hissed quietly into the smartphone in her hand, "I'm not going to do that!" There was a pause while the other person spoke. "Look, I can't do it any faster than I am without getting caught, and I haven't told anyone!" Maxim heard a sad sigh. "Ok. I understand. I'll do the last one as soon as I get a chance. Don't... Just *don't*, okay? I'll do it."

Maxim held in a gasp. Who was on the other end of the phone, and what did they want Doctor Llewellyn to do? Was she involved with the saboteurs? Why would she refuse to follow orders if she was one of them? Perhaps the person on the other end of the call was threatening her in some way.

Maxim was torn, unsure what he should do. He couldn't go to John or Jean with his suspicions, not yet. He couldn't accuse an esteemed TQB scientist of colluding with the enemy without hard evidence.

He crept away from the door and resumed his patrol. This would have to wait until tonight, when he could discuss it with the others.

United Kingdom, North Wales, Conwy Castle, King's Tower, Student Dormitory

There was a heavenly aroma in the air as the students piled into the dormitory at the end of the day—real Earth food. Tina thought the smell rivaled even Chef Van's cooking.

Doctor Llewellyn stood at the kitchenette counter with John, emptying the contents of ten pizza boxes onto plates. Ice-cold bottles of sugar-free soda stood on the draining board, dripping condensation onto the towel beneath them.

"Pizza!" Tina rushed over to the counter with the others to grab a soda and her plate of cheesy deliciousness and a hug from her uncle.

"This one's yours, Teeny." John grinned, pushing one of the plates toward her. "Plain cheese, just how you always have it."

Tina let go of John and took the plate from him, then went over to sit at the table with Maxim, who was sitting alone and brooding. The pizza filled the plate from edge to edge, and was cut in handy squares. She picked a slice up eagerly, watching the hot cheese stretch with anticipation.

The cheese finally broke, and she blew on the slice before taking a big bite. "Mmmm," she said when she'd finished chewing. "Just how I like it. There's nothing like cheese pizza done well."

"I'll tell the guys at the Bay Grill you said so," Doctor Llewellyn said from the kitchenette with a wink.

Maxim looked up at the sound of her voice, his eyes narrowing ever so slightly. Tina didn't miss it. "What's up, Maxim?"

He avoided her questioning gaze, speaking so quietly she could barely hear him. "Not now, Tina. Wait until lights out, then we can talk. Bring Ron, okay?"

Tina lowered her voice. "Are you okay?"

Maxim hushed her, his eyes darting over to the counter where Doctor Llewellyn spoke to John about the history of the castle and the surrounding area. "*Da*, I am fine, but something strange is going on here. We will talk later."

The subject was definitely closed when Maxim's tablet started buzzing. "Nestor!" he cried, dashing off to the sleeping area to take the call. "Hey, Tina, come on," he called over his shoulder. "Yana is on the call too. Get Ron!"

Tina hauled Ron away from the pizza at the counter. "Yana and Nestor are calling, so come on!"

Ron took a last slice and followed her.

Maxim was just plugging a lead into the TV to transfer the call to the big screen when the other two flopped down on the sofa.

Yana waved as soon as she saw them, grinning from ear to ear. "Hey!"

Nestor was practically vibrating with excitement. "You will not believe what I have been doing today!"

"Tell us!" Maxim cried, happy to see his cousin.

Nestor launched into a rundown of the things he'd been

learning that week. "But the best part was going out to the asteroid field and shooting at the rocks!"

Ron and Maxim were practically drooling.

Yana had news as well. "Our little werecat is doing better with each day. I have been teaching him English, with Meredith's help."

Talk turned to lighter things, and Tina drifted back over to the kitchenette for another slice of pizza. For the rest of the evening she watched Doctor Llewellyn. She appeared to be nice enough, but Maxim's suspicious behavior toward the doctor made Tina look at her in a different light.

Her happiness was a show for their benefit, Tina decided. Every now and then the happy mask would slip while John's back was turned and Tina got a glimpse of a woman in turmoil. She and Yana had taken Negotiation together as an elective. The class had taught her that politics weren't for her, but she had learned to spot a faker a mile away. Doctor Llewellyn was hiding *something*, for certain.

The moment the adults left for the night she cornered Maxim. "Start talking," she demanded. "*I* think Doctor Llewellyn is hiding something. What do you know?"

The others were drawn to the tone of her voice, and the students gathered around Maxim's bunk to hear his tale.

"Do you think she's involved with the saboteur?" Ron asked after Maxim had finished recounting Doctor Llewellyn's side of the conversation. "She seems so nice!"

Maxim's agony showed on his face. "I cannot help but think that after what I heard, but I do not believe she is acting of her own free will. That's why I did not go straight to John. If I am right and she is being coerced—"

"She might have a family," Aleksi whispered. "We don't know."

A hush fell over the group. Even those who hadn't been on the bus when terrorists trying to get at Bethany Anne had kidnapped them knew what had gone down that fateful day. The Romanovkan kids had all heard the story of how their leader, Boris, had turned on the kidnappers and assisted the Patriarch in returning them to their families.

The loss of Michael weighed heavily upon everyone who loved the Queen. Her loss was *their* loss, too, and they were old enough to understand the consequences of being careless when lives were on the line.

It made them think.

"We need to find proof, one way or another," Masha said firmly.

Aleksi disagreed. "You heard Ms. Dukes, no poking around. We should tell her what Maxim heard and let the adults deal with it."

Tina considered it for a moment. "We don't have much of anything to tell her. We could be wrong, what if she was just having an argument with someone?"

"It was more than an argument, Tina," Maxim told her. "She sounded sad, but also afraid."

Ron was unhappy. "Look, we could be wrong, and then we'll be in trouble for making accusations. You know how busy Ms. Dukes is, she doesn't need us distracting her with conspiracy theories."

"Wow, you sounded just like your mom then, Ron" Tina

snickered. "We can find some evidence, then we're not wasting anyone's time."

"I just want to make sure we're doing the right thing," he replied. "If someone has kidnapped her family, who's to say they're not watching?"

Masha waved his concerns off. "All the more reason for us to do the sleuthing. If there is someone watching then they won't be paying attention to us. All they'll see is a bunch of kids. Let's take advantage of that. We're nearly adults now, Ron. Now's our chance to step up and help out. We've got this."

Tina nodded. "If she is being blackmailed in some way, she needs our help. If not, we expose her to John and Ms. Dukes. Then they will be focused on what we are bringing, and not on punishing us for disobeying them."

Ron shrugged. "If that's what everyone wants then I'm in. I just wanted to be sure we all knew what we were doing."

Tina patted his shoulder. "I know. We aren't going to rush in, we'll make a plan and stick to it."

"Where do we start?" Maxim asked.

"We should search her quarters," Mischa suggested.

"Or her office. That would be less risky," Halli put in. "We could cause a distraction while one of you techy wizards searches her computer and her phone."

Craig jumped in. "I could pull the fire alarm? They'd totally believe I'd do that for a prank. Then you three can slip into the office and find the evidence. I can take the heat."

Tina ran the idea through in her mind. "It could work.

But if we *do* find evidence she's being blackmailed, we'll take it to my uncle and let him handle it. Deal?"

The two hours before lights out were spent planning in detail how to get in and out of Doctor Llewellyn's office without being caught. After that, Tina lay in bed trying to find a flaw in their plan. She couldn't see one, but that didn't mean there weren't any. A thought occurred to her just as her eyes fluttered shut, but it was lost to dreams in which she was chased through the castle by umbrella-wielding monsters wearing bowler hats.

The next morning...

"Are we really going to do this?" Ron whispered, his nervous breath tickling the back of Tina's neck. She jumped, which rustled the foliage in front of her.

"Shhh, they'll hear you," she hissed back, pushing them both farther behind the potted ferns they were using for cover. They were waiting for Doctor Llewellyn and Jean to leave the office in the remodeled visitor's center.

Ron snickered nervously. "If they catch us, we could just say we were making out."

Tina arched an eyebrow. "You want to tell my uncle we were making out?" She snorted gently. "Your funeral. Be my guest."

Ron paled at the thought of what John would do to any boy foolish enough to admit to such a thing. "You're right. On second thought, let's not do that."

"Uh huh." Tina saw shadows moving behind the frosted glass pane in the door and pushed him back farther into the corner. "Shhh, they're leaving. Send the signal!"

Ron tapped his tablet, and a few seconds later the fire alarm began to shriek. The adults came out of the office, Jean looking up and around for danger. Doctor Llewellyn locked the door behind them. She paused to put the big brass key in the pocket of her lab coat.

Tina noticed it was the same one the doctor had been wearing the day before. For a second she thought Jean had seen them behind the potted plants, but she must have imagined it because her teacher followed Doctor Llewellyn when she hurried out through the front door a moment later.

Tina smiled to herself; Step One was complete. She spoke at normal volume, the alarm covering the sound. "Ron, has Aleksi taken care of the cameras?"

He looked down at the screen again. "Yes, we're good to go as soon as Masha gets here. Did she ever tell you the story of why she learned to pick locks? It's a suspicious skill to have, if you ask me."

"Concentrate, Ron," Tina admonished him. "We're on a clock here."

Ron's tablet buzzed in his hand. "Oh, geez. My tablet just died!"

"Seriously? Not the best time. Here, use mine." She passed him her tablet and refocused on the section of corridor Masha was due to arrive from any moment now.

Masha appeared in the next minute and Tina relaxed. Step Two was underway.

"I nearly didn't make it," Masha said breathlessly. "I bumped into Doctor Llewellyn and Jean. They wanted me to go with them, but I told them I had orders to report to John. I think they bought it."

"It won't hold for long. We need to get in there before they all meet up and notice we're missing!" Ron exclaimed. "Will we even have time to get into the office before someone comes searching for us?"

"No worries, Ronnie." Masha grinned. "I snagged this when I bumped into the Doctor." She held up a burnished key and waved it in front of his nose.

"No *way*!" Ron didn't try to hide his shock. "You picked her pocket? Not cool, Masha."

"In this instance it's not a bad thing," Tina said. "Think of what could be at stake here, Ron. Come on, we're wasting time." She took the key and unlocked the office door, urging the two of them to get inside so she could close it.

Once inside she took stock of the spartan office, murmuring to herself, "Where would I hide evidence if I were a saboteur…?"

"On the computer, obviously," Masha offered.

"Not her TQB computer," Tina retorted. "Otherwise ADAM would see it."

Ron nodded. His dad had been one of the team who'd created ADAM, so he knew more than most about the AI.

"ADAM?" Masha asked.

"Oh, um. He's like the computer guy." Tina forgot that only some people knew about the digital entity she thought of as an honorary uncle.

Masha wrinkled her nose. "Right, so not on her TQB computer. So where do *you* think she'd hide the evidence, then?"

"You could start with her desk." Ron was already searching through a filing cabinet, one drawer at a time.

There was nothing on the desk except a pen holder and a silver-framed photograph of Doctor Llewellyn with what Tina assumed was her family. She had her arm around the man next to her, and each of them had a small child under the other arm. They looked happy, Tina thought.

It was strange Doctor Llewellyn hadn't mentioned having kids when they were eating last night.

They followed Ron's suggestion, quickly finding that the drawers were locked.

"It's a pity we don't have the keys to this as well," Tina moaned.

"No problem," Masha said, snagging a couple of paper-clips from the desk.

She unfolded the first and made a loop with the second, which she inserted into the lock. She wiggled it a couple of times and smiled, pushing the unfolded clip in beside it. After few deft jerks, Tina heard the lock click.

"Great job, Masha!" she gushed, hope returned. She rummaged carefully through the drawer while Masha moved on to the next lock.

The top drawers held nothing of interest, but the double drawer at the bottom clunked as Tina pulled it open. She peered inside but it was empty.

"It can't be empty!" she cried. "I just heard something move in there!"

Ron came over and leaned down to get a better look. "Oh, *cool*. Take a closer look…what's wrong with that drawer?"

Tina calmed herself and looked again, and it hit her. "It's bigger on the outside. It's a false drawer!"

Just then the fire alarm cut out. The three froze and

exchanged horrified glances.

Tina was first to react. "Quick, Ron. How do we get it open?"

Ron ran his fingers around the bottom of the drawer. He pressed and probed until there was a click and the false bottom came free.

A smartphone lay underneath, and Tina put it in her pocket.

Ron replaced the false bottom carefully. "Come on, let's get out of here. Doctor Llewellyn will be back any minute."

They waited another minute while Masha finished locking the last drawer and went to the door, opening it a crack.

Too late. Doctor Llewellyn walked in and stopped dead when she saw them standing around her desk looking guilty.

"What are you doing in my office?" Doctor Llewellyn's soft musical voice held a sharp note. "Jean has people searching the castle for you!"

Ron held his tablet up sheepishly. "I needed a charger for this. Sorry, Doctor Llewellyn."

She narrowed her eyes. "Hmmm. How did you get in? I locked the door behind me when the fire alarm went off."

Masha held up the key. "This was in the door, ma'am."

Doctor Llewellyn looked flustered. "Is that so? I'll be having a chat with Jean about this, mark my words. Off you go, now. Get yourselves to your dorm."

They stood there, not knowing what to do. Tina was terrified that the smartphone would ring and give them away. She surreptitiously thumbed the power button, giving it a long press to switch it off.

Doctor Llewellyn shook her head in disbelief. "Why are you still here? Well? Off you go!"

They didn't need to be told again.

They pelted out of the office and up the corridor, continuing their mad dash until they were in the safety of the dorm room to which the others had been sent after Craig had confessed to pulling the alarm.

United Kingdom, North Wales, Undisclosed Location

Broadbent watched as one of the bank of monitors on the wall showed Laura Llewellyn shooing the TQB kids from her office.

The analyst was clearly concerned. "Looks like they found the phone we gave to Doctor Llewellyn, sir. It was switched on and off again whilst the doctor was away from her office."

Broadbent nodded brusquely. "Looks like they did, Perkins. Those bloody kids are cleverer than they look. Tracking is in place though, yes?"

"Yes sir. If they switch it on again we'll know."

"What about the cameras, did we manage to get one in the dormitory?"

"No, sir. Doctor Llewellyn refused point-blank to do it."

"Damn it! We're losing control of this. We'll just have to move the timetable up and go to Plan B, Perkins. Put it in motion immediately."

Perkins pursed his lips. "Sir, are you certain this course of action is necessary? I must say, I'm not keen on the idea of John Grimes turning up at our front door in a tizzy."

"I agree, Perkins, but needs must when the Devil drives.

We have a duty to fulfill. Move the Llewellyn family to the black site."

Perkins nodded as he typed. "If they get into that phone John Grimes is going to go on the warpath, sir. You know what TQB does to kidnappers. We all saw the reports from Vegas and Colorado. Gave me nightmares for weeks."

"It's not *if*, Perkins, it's *when*. We have been left to bear the brunt of piss-poor management. As usual, all we can do is try to complete our objective and make sure the collateral damage is minimal so Whitehall can cover it up. Get them to the mine, and make sure there are enough guards to keep even John Grimes busy."

Broadbent wasn't done. "Now, where are my Special Forces? I want them ready to move in as soon as John Grimes leaves to rescue the Llewellyns."

"Yes, sir." Perkins clicked his mouse a couple of times. "They've been held up, it seems."

He let his incredulity show in his reply. "What? You're joking, surely? I didn't think anything held those SAS lads up."

"That's what Intelligence is telling me," Perkins confirmed. "There's a weather front preventing any flights from leaving Joint Helicopter Command. They're coming by boat instead."

"Well, hurry them up!" Broadbent couldn't hide the weary edge in his voice.

"They will be here in an hour or so, sir," Perkins told him.

"I suppose that's better than nothing. Keep monitoring the feeds, and let me know if anything changes." Broadbent sighed as the telephone began to shrill in his office.

CHAPTER NINE

United Kingdom, North Wales, Conwy Castle, East Barbican

Maxim struggled to stay focused on Craig as they sparred. His mind was on the lies they had told. It was not sitting well with him to be a part of dishonesty like this.

Craig had blocked him twice, and now scored a point with a tap to Maxim's ribs.

"Come on, dude!" Craig said under his breath so only Maxim could hear. "Nothing's going to give the game away like John's star student getting his butt handed to him by little old me!"

"Keep your guard up, Maxim," John called from where he sat on a stone, watching the students spar.

"See?" Craig put a little more effort into his next attack. "If *I'm* the one telling you to focus, you need to pull it in." The look on Craig's face was pure delight as he scored another half-point.

Maxim growled, as much in disgust at himself as at

Craig. "I think not." He pushed aside the thoughts of the smartphone hidden in the dorm and defended for real. "I'm surprised you can still move after all the pushups you got for pulling the alarm."

Craig skipped out of Maxim's reach, flexing his biceps as a distraction for the leg sweep he came in with. "Can't contain awesome like this, Maxim. There's just too much of it!"

They were well matched, if not evenly so. He wasn't quite as big as Craig, but then there was a good year between them. While Craig was ahead in age, size and confidence, Maxim had the advantage of time spent watching the Guardians train around the APAs whenever he'd had a break, and the payoff from hounding his Uncle Leonid to spar with him until the reluctant Guardian agreed to help him learn.

Craig's grin went up a thousand watts when he realized they were truly testing each other now. He went in with a knee-stamp that Maxim deflected, following up his block with a jab to Craig's abdomen. He controlled his strength, never hitting harder than was necessary to score a point.

Craig kept up the pace, parrying the punches and kicks. He threw his own here and there, but he was getting more joy out of seeing Maxim's techniques.

It cost him the bout. Maxim scored five points in quick succession, hitting the target John had set before the start of the match.

"Geez!" Craig exclaimed with the last one, a stinging flick to the nose.

Maxim grinned, flushed with adrenaline. "*Da*, good. You will think twice before annoying me again."

John intervened. "Switch partners. Craig, you're with Mischa. Masha, you're with Hallie. Maxim, you're with me."

Maxim paled. He was going to spar with John? What if John could read minds, like it was rumored all the Queen's inner circle could do?

John smiled at him. "Relax. I liked what you did there. Peter tells me you've been hanging around the APAs a lot since you last came down here. You're picking it up quickly."

"Thank you, sir. I want to learn so I can protect my friends and family. So I can protect my father, if I ever find him."

"Still no news of him?"

Maxim shook his head sadly. "No, sir. Every day I ask Meredith, and every day she says there has been no sighting."

John patted his shoulder. "If he's down here, we'll find him. You're going to make a great Guardian, Maxim. In the meantime, I'll arrange for you to take a class with Peter so you can keep upping your martial arts game. "

Maxim's ears fizzed and his heart beat hard for two or three pumps. He was sure that at any moment John would ask him why he was so nervous all of a sudden. "Thank you, sir," he managed through a dry mouth.

"You can thank yourself. Using your initiative always pays off. What's that quote on the wall in the Academy? 'As long as a student pushes themselves…' That applies to all of us, not just the Queen. You pushed for knowledge, so here I am to open the door."

The secret twisted knots in his stomach as Maxim struggled to speak. "I will do my best."

John patted his shoulder. "That's all anyone can do, buddy."

CHAPTER TEN

Q BBS *Meredith Reynolds*, **Medical Wing**

Bai Hu sat up in bed. His face lit up as he tasted ice cream for the first time in his life. "*Tiánměi*, Yana! *Mmmmm!*"

Yana didn't need Meredith to translate. She could see the joy the treat brought the little werecat. "You like it?"

He dug the spoon in to snag another delicious mouthful. "*Xièxiè!* I like. This is?"

Yana had to think for a moment to work out the meaning of his question. "Oh, ice cream." She pointed to it as she said the words, "This is ice cream."

"'Ice cream.'" He launched into a stream of impossibly fast Chinese she had no hope of understanding. He saw the lost look on her face and pointed at the ceiling. "Meredith."

"Good idea," she said.

Meredith had already heard her name. "Hello, children. Do you need my assistance again?"

"Yes please, Meredith. Can you tell me what Bai Hu is saying? If you have time," Yana asked politely.

"I always have time for the children, Yana. I find my interactions with younger humans extremely rewarding."

She repeated herself in Chinese for Bai Hu, something Yana and Bai Hu had not asked the EI to do. Yana appreciated Meredith's initiative. It had gone a long way toward breaking down the language barrier between them. Little by little, Bai Hu was coming out of his shell.

Bai Hu spoke to Meredith. Yana was beginning to recognize a phrase here and there, things Bai Hu repeated often enough that her sharp mind picked them up.

"Bai Hu says that he has never tasted anything so sweet as the ice cream, Yana. He is comparing this day to a religious celebration where gifts are given and expressing his regret that he has nothing to give you in return."

Yana smiled and wrapped an arm around Bai Hu's shoulder. "The gift is having a chance to know you, Bai Hu."

When Meredith translated this for him he pushed his over-bed table away and returned her hug with feeling, burying his head against her shoulder and crying with a mixture of grief and happiness.

He started to speak, but paused and then tried his best to say it in his halting English. "You...my... *yīngxióng*... good person. I die with no Yana."

She hugged him even tighter. "I would never let that happen. Thank you, Meredith."

"You are welcome, Yana," Meredith replied. "Your father is outside the room. I will leave you to enjoy the good news he is bringing."

Before Yana could ask Meredith what the news was the door opened and Nicholas entered the room, struggling with his arms full of brightly wrapped packages, a basket filled with fruit and cupcakes, and a bunch of balloons.

She rushed to help him, taking the top three packages and placing them on the table next to Bai Hu's bed. "What is all this, Father?"

Her father grinned. "These are all gifts sent to Bai Hu by the Queen's people to wish him welcome and a speedy recovery." He repeated himself in Chinese for Bai Hu, who looked at the mound of presents with an awestruck expression.

"Open them!" Nicholas beamed, miming tearing the paper.

Bai Hu did not need to be told twice. He began with the smallest package, carefully opening it without making a single tear in the tiger-print giftwrap. He cocked his head inquisitively at the pair of socks inside.

"That is not all, children. The doctor has assured me that Bai Hu will be discharged from the medical wing tomorrow."

Yana had been both expecting and dreading this news. "Is he really coming to live with us, Papa?" she asked, her eyes suddenly full of stinging tears. "I couldn't bear it if the Queen changed her mind. I want us to take care of him always."

Her father nodded. "This is why the Queen has entrusted him to our care, my love. I signed the paperwork before I came here. If Bai Hu agrees, we will be his new family."

The little werecat listened solemnly as her father translated. When Nicholas finished he sat in silence for a minute, his hands folded in his lap and his head down.

When he looked up, he nodded at Nicholas as he spoke. She recognized the words for "yes," and "thank you," but the rest was lost as began to sob.

Yana laid a hand on his shoulder.

"Are you okay?"

Bai Hu looked up at her, his dark eyes sad. "I miss mama."

Yana couldn't hold back her tears any longer. "I miss my mama, too."

She gathered the boy in her arms, and Nicholas embraced them both to comfort them.

"We will heal our wounds together," he said, kissing each of them on the head. "We will make each other strong, my children."

Yana laughed. "You are a father again!"

"And you will have the little brother you always asked for." He put a hand on each of their cheeks, bending to look them in the eyes. He spoke first in Chinese, then in Russian. "We will honor your mothers by living happy lives, although we will never forget those we have lost. They are always in our hearts."

He stood and picked the biggest, shiniest gift from the pile.

"Now, let's see what is in all these packages. Are you ready to open the next one, my son?"

United Kingdom, North Wales, King's Tower, Student Dormitory

They all sat around Tina, looking at the smartphone with a mixture of excitement and worry.

"Shall I switch it on?" She looked at the assembled students with doubt on her face.

Craig grimaced. "We need to know what's on that phone."

Tina touched the power button, but drew her finger back before committing to pressing it. "What if they can track it? Whoever 'they' are."

Maxim shared her concern. "If it is true that Doctor Llewellyn is being coerced, we cannot risk alerting the blackmailers to our discovery." He put his head in his hands. "I do not want to be responsible for making things worse if we are discovered."

"*Da*, Maxim is right," Masha concurred. "It would be foolish to assume we will not get caught. What if the doctor is not being blackmailed at all? What if she is working *with* these bad guys against TQB? She could make things very difficult for us. We all heard what Ms. Dukes said—they all want our tech. Bad guys don't just quit because there are kids around."

Ron had a thought. "They must be after Project Gauntlet, the new armor-making process."

Aleksi nodded vehemently. "Yes, that must be it. But maybe not all..." He became lost in his tablet for a moment, holding it up for everyone to see the results of his search. "Here, see? Doctor Llewellyn's process is being used to make components for weapons, also. But not at this site. Maybe the bad guys don't know that? I vote we turn the phone on."

"Me too," Halli agreed.

There were nods from Craig and Mischa.

"How are you accessing all this information, Aleksi? That looked like a classified document."

"Oh, I am connected to the *Meredith Reynolds*, I just asked nicely. The system EI usually allows me to look at stuff as long as I explain why I need it. It is really intuitive, even for an EI."

Tina and Ron exchanged a quick glance. They knew that Aleksi's skills must have been noticed by ADAM if he was getting access like that.

Aleksi went over to his bunk and grabbed his charger cable from the nightstand, plugging it into his tablet. He came back over and held his hand out for the smartphone. "We will copy it and look at the contents that way. Here, I'll do it through my tablet."

"NO!" Ron and Tina cried in unison.

Ron explained. "Activity like that on one of our tablets would be flagged by Meredith immediately." Only Tina knew that he was more concerned about being busted by ADAM.

The others were perplexed.

"Trust us," Tina assured. "The last thing we want is Ms. Dukes and my uncle finding out we did all this before we have proof."

"So I shouldn't search for the phone's model number, either." He put his tablet down.

"So what are we going to do?" Masha rubbed her tired eyes.

Maxim stood and stretched. "We are going to get some sleep, and come at it from a different angle tomorrow. Let us hide the phone. Maybe one of the stones can be loosened? Then it is safe until we are decided."

"Good idea," Tina agreed. "It's late, and we have a full day of pulling machinery apart scheduled tomorrow."

"John said we're going climbing after breakfast." Halli yawned as she spoke. "Apparently we're driving him up the wall, and he wants to return the favor."

That brought chuckles from them all as they broke apart and prepared for bed.

As she lay waiting to fall asleep Tina couldn't stop thinking about the kids in the photograph on Doctor Llewellyn's desk. Were they in danger? She had to find out, and stop whatever was going on here.

United Kingdom, North Wales, Conwy Castle, East Barbican

It was five thirty in the morning, and John had gathered the five Wechselbalg on the grass on the King's Tower side of the barbican. The wall of the tower had been fitted with a climbing wall during the renovation of the castle and the kids would soon be scaling it.

Maxim craned his neck to see where the crenellations blocked out the morning sun. Ron had told him the towers were just over twenty meters tall, made from reinforced stone. The climbing wall was split down the middle by a series of platforms with a ladder on each side for those who had reached their limit. The result was two identical routes to the top, and the holds changed color at each platform as the difficulty of the climb increased.

"This is perfect for a race," Maxim remarked quietly to himself. He would usually say these kinds of things to

Nestor. It was strange to be so far away from his cousin for so long. "I miss you, brother," he murmured.

Craig's sensitive hearing picked it up and he nudged Maxim with his shoulder. "Hey, you okay? Are you up for a race? I'm not your cousin, but I'll be your buddy."

Maxim nodded stiffly, saved from an emotional response to Craig's words by John calling them to attention.

John paced in front of them with his hands behind his back. "Good morning, class. Your first challenge should not be a challenge at all. You've all had time on the walls at school, and this is just the same—just on a larger scale."

None of them were impressed, despite the height of the wall.

John had a twinkle in his eye. "This is just the warm-up. We're going free-climbing as soon as I'm assured that everyone has their sensible head on today." He looked directly at Craig for a long moment. "If everyone does, we'll make a day of it. The whole town is surrounded by walls. Let's see if we can have some fun and challenge ourselves! This afternoon we'll work on surveillance. I've heard there's a few nice places to eat in town, so we're going people watching while we get some lunch."

Maxim and the others whooped for joy. They had been working hard since they arrived at the castle, getting a glimpse of their future lives as Guardians. The situation with Doctor Llewellyn was also weighing on their minds. A little fun and some physical exertion were just what they needed.

"That's more like it," John exclaimed. He picked up a

bowl of chalk from the equipment stand and held it out. "Maxim and Craig, you're up first."

Maxim dipped his hands in the chalk and rubbed them together. "Are you ready to race, my friend?" he asked Craig.

"You bet your furry butt I am!" he replied smartly.

They lined up side by side, ready to go on John's signal.

He gave a whistle and they raced to the tower, both boys leaping as high up the wall as they could to catch a jug hold to get a head start on the race. John and the girls cheered them on, spurring them both to greater speeds.

Maxim kept his eyes on the section of the wall above, plotting the most efficient route as he went. The first part of the wall was easy, Maxim found plenty of holds evenly spaced, and the wall was textured to make it easy to grip with his feet. It was ideal for beginners, and no trouble whatsoever for an energetic young Wechselbalg.

He powered up the wall, and Craig was right beside him the whole time. Maxim did not watch his rival's progress out of the corner of his eye. Instead, he focused on looking up toward the mid-portion of the wall, which was where things began to get interesting.

As soon as they passed the first platform, the wall transformed under his hands. The easy grips were gone, and the boys had to work to find the next one instead of being given the multiple options they'd had on the first section.

"How's it going over there?" Craig called from a hair's breadth below him.

Maxim grunted and kept pushing himself upward.

The third section of the wall increased in difficulty again. As well as the reduction in available grips, the wall was no longer flat. Stones jutted, creating overhangs the boys had to scramble up and around. There were no more platforms after this, and the two routes merged into one wall for the last ten feet.

Maxim saw the slip before it happened.

He reached across and grabbed Craig's arm, enabling the older Wechselbalg to get a grip again before he fell off the tower.

Maxim didn't think the fall would have killed a Wechselbalg, but it would have left Craig stuck in medical —*again*. They heaved themselves over the top and stood panting, holding themselves upright with their hands on their thighs as the adrenaline dissipated.

Craig grinned and held up a hand as he caught his breath. "Duuude, that was *epic*! I love teaming up with you. I always push myself that little bit harder!"

This time Maxim reciprocated Craig's high-five. Maxim was coming to realize that Craig could be a loyal friend and staunch ally. They were a good match physically, and any problems Craig's seniority might have caused Maxim's alpha tendencies were dispelled by Craig's sunny nature and the solid character his joking disguised.

He pulled Craig into a backslapping hug. "You challenge me also, my friend. It is good to be your teammate."

Craig grinned again. "Come on, let's see who's next."

An hour later, John was satisfied that all the students had sufficient climbing skills to be let loose on a real wall. They all piled into one of the facility's vehicles—a silver Land Rover Sport with tinted windows—and waited for John to return from the castle kitchen.

He came back carrying three bulging kitbags and a

cooler—with ease. He put everything in the back before climbing into the driver's seat.

"There's rain forecast for this afternoon," John said casually. "Looks like the people-watching is cancelled."

The girls groaned as one.

"What about lunch?" Craig asked hopefully. They could all smell the food John had put in the trunk.

"What about climbing?" Halli added.

"We're going out to Snowdonia to camp for the night instead. Doctor Llewellyn told me about a place you kids can really work off some steam." He hooked a thumb toward the back of the car. "I think you can all smell your lunch. Fair warning, dinner will not be as delicious as lunch."

"What?" Halli's face was incredulous. "Will we have to *hunt?*"

John laughed. "You can if you want to. I was thinking we'd just eat the food substitutes I brought, but if you'd rather eat rabbit we can do that instead."

"My vote is for pizza," Mischa said quickly, trying to negotiate.

"Mine too!" Masha agreed. "Who knows when we'll get to eat real pizza again after this trip?"

"I think we *all* vote for pizza!" Craig concurred.

"Maybe there will be somewhere we can stop and get some takeout," John conceded.

Maxim hoped they weren't going to be driving for long. The food smelled good, and breakfast was only a distant memory in his teenage Wechselbalg mind. John drove them out of the parking lot and through the security barriers at both ends of the tunnel leading out of the facility grounds.

Maxim blinked at the rapid change in the light levels as they crested the dip at the tunnel exit. The steel gray sky was jarring after the dimly-lit tunnel.

The journey passed quickly. He leaned against the front passenger-side window as they drove through the country-side. Craig and the girls were in the back, laughing and pointing out the road signs as they saw them. Each tried to outdo the others with outlandish attempts to pronounce the Welsh words as they went.

"You okay, buddy?" John asked from driver's seat. "You're quiet today."

Maxim looked over at John for a moment before returning to watching the sheep and the trees go by. "I am fine, thank you, sir."

"Hmm-mm," John murmured, focusing on the road and giving Maxim time to put what he was thinking into words.

"I think I have been unkind to Craig," he said softly. "I dismissed him as a fool, but he has more depth than that. I am ashamed of myself for being judgmental."

"So you should be! I'm *awesome*!" Craig yelled from the back of the car, pounding the back of Maxim's seat with his fists.

Maxim groaned. "And then he behaves like this and I want to throttle him!"

John laughed heartily. "Looks like you found your Tabitha!"

"Hey!" Craig began to protest. "Actually, I'll take that. Ranger Two is *B.A.D.A.S.S.* When I grow up I wanna be *just* like her!"

The whole car burst into laughter as they crossed the bridge at Betws-Y-Coed and headed into Snowdonia.

United Kingdom, North Wales, Snowdonia National Park, Swallow Falls

"Perkins! Answer the comm, damn you!" Broadbent was having a miserable time playing tourist. He had been hanging around the falls for the last couple of hours while he waited for the SAS contact he was meeting to appear.

"Sorry, sir," Perkins sounded excited. "I was just confirming a report from Doctor Llewellyn. It seems John Grimes has left the castle, sir."

Broadbent grinned, startling some young lovebirds enjoying the romance of the day as his mouth performed the unfamiliar movement. "Jolly good! Perhaps he's going to sod off back to space and let us get on with things, eh?"

This could be the turning of the tide for this absolute bollocks of an operation, he thought.

"Oh," was all Perkins said in reply.

"What do you mean by 'oh?'"

Perkins gulped loud enough to be heard over the comm. "Erm...sir? He's headed your way."

Broadbent had to take control of his body before it betrayed him. He took a firm grip on the tree beside him. "As in, 'he knows who I am and he's headed my way to end me?'" His knees went to jelly, and his stomach threatened to eject the rum-raisin ice cream he'd eaten instead of lunch.

"Looks that way, sir. Satellite has him getting into a

vehicle with five others at the castle and driving to Betws-Y-Coed. Looks like they're headed into Snowdonia."

The last time Broadbent had been this afraid, he had been crouched in the burnt shell of a ruined building while the bombs exploded around him. Now, as then, he felt naked and exposed. He shrank back, suddenly certain that anyone who looked at him would be able to *see* the terror pouring out of him. This was beyond fight or flight. He had taken those children, and he knew what would happen when John Grimes found him.

He only hoped that he could face his death with more bravery than he'd shown in this moment.

"Sir." Perkins interrupted his thoughts. "I've managed to clean up the image from the castle car park a fair bit. I may have jumped the gun a little, sir. John Grimes is escorting five of the TQB children."

Relief hit Broadbent like a hammer, and he released a breath he hadn't realized he'd been holding. "Looks like we get to live another day, Perkins. He wouldn't take kids to an execution."

"Jolly good, sir. Retirement is looking rather attractive at the moment, I must say." Perkins signed off.

"I couldn't agree more," Broadbent muttered to himself. The young couple looked at him strangely again.

Time to move on. It wouldn't do to be remembered if John Grimes *did* turn up and start asking questions. If only the SAS chap would hurry up!

A muddy four-wheel drive pulled up beside him, polluting the air with thrashing guitar music. Damn kids. Broadbent wrinkled his nose as the window wound down and a head popped out. "Broadbent?"

He nodded to the driver, who flashed his ID, confirming he was the contact Broadbent had been waiting for.

"Get in if you will, sir. We haven't got all day!"

He sighed as he got into the passenger side of the beat-up vehicle.

The driver held out a hand for Broadbent to shake. "Corporal Sykes, sir. Nice to meet you. So...what's it like, being a spook?"

Broadbent pursed his lips and shrugged. "Nothing like the telly shows, that's for sure. Where are we headed?"

Sykes looked askance at him. "We're bivvied a short way into the forest, sir. Have I offended you in any way? You don't seem pleased to be here."

Broadbent shook his head. "It's been a long couple of weeks, that's all. You don't look like an AC/DC fan, Sykes. Bit before your time, I would say."

Sykes grinned, the action making him look even younger to Broadbent's weary eyes. "Oh, I loves the old bands, sir. My dad was an SAS man before me, and his unit had all the hits recorded for when they went into the theatre. You want me to turn it off?"

Broadbent shook his head again. "No, you're all right, lad. Leave it on."

They listened in silence as they drove. The road gave way to a lane, and the lane led to a dirt track through the forest that culminated in a muddy clearing full of similarly distressed-looking vehicles.

"What's with all the cars?" Broadbent asked.

"We don't want TQB spotting us, so everyone drove in by a different route once we left Anglesey. We're all playing tourist; it's the perfect cover in Wales. Everyone who's not a local is a tourist at this time of year."

A beefy man wearing a rugby shirt approached. "Agent Broadbent, is it?"

Broadbent nodded, showing his ID.

"Good to have you with us." He held out a chunky hand for Broadbent to shake. "Captain Myerscough, at your service. Now, tell me about what we're up against here. All I have is speculation. I'm surrounded by a bunch of wet-nosed sissies who are too scared of the boogeyman to do their jobs properly!"

This time Broadbent kept the sigh inside. It wouldn't do to be disrespectful to the man commanding the hundred-strong unit before the assault on the castle.

"John Grimes is here, sir. I'm sure you've heard of him?"

"Not really, Broadbent, I've only ever heard of one John Grimes, and it *can't* be him."

Broadbent nodded to the captain.

Bradley paled. "*That* John Grimes is *here*? Who is running this shambles?"

"That would be you, sir," Broadbent said with a rueful smile. "I'm just here to liaise."

Captain Myerscough began bellowing orders at the soldiers standing around, and within twenty minutes there were a number of small recon teams scrambling to leave.

CHAPTER ELEVEN

Q BBS *Meredith Reynolds*, Etheric Academy, Administration Office

"What do you mean you've got a date?" Diane squealed. "Don't tell me you got that pilot to ask you out!" She adjusted the phone against her ear and scooched into a more comfortable position to receive the gossip.

"I did!" Dorene whooped. "Better yet, he has a handsome friend and I set *you* up, too! Hang on, I'll be at the office in a moment. Put the kettle on, would you, dear?"

Dorene swept through the door just as Diane placed two steaming-hot mugs on the table. She pushed the Earl Grey tea toward Dorene and blew on her coffee while she waited for her sister to get settled.

"*DJ*! So, when is our date? It will be a double, won't it?"

"Everything's double with *us*, my dear!" Dorene wiggled an eyebrow, making Diane choke on the donut she'd just dunked in her coffee. "It's tomorrow night, at All Guns Blazing."

"Ooh, it's been so long since we've been on a date! I *told* you apologizing to Jean would make it all better." Diane ignored the sour look from her sister. "Are you sure about dating a pilot, though? It didn't go so well last time."

When she opened the attachment Dorene had sent, it was not the handsome pilot face she expected. "Not the roster!"

"Yes, the roster." Dorene smirked. "Not all pilots are arrogant jerks. Anyway, *you* promised not to bring up the butt-pinching incident again if I apologized to Jean, and we can't go meet Thomas and Leonard tomorrow night if we don't get our work done."

Diane blushed. "Sorry, DJ. Ok, let's do the roster—but not because you're punishing me for a slip of the tongue. What's on the agenda tonight?"

Dorene flicked her tablet and the roster jumped to the holo-projector on the desk. "First is Jean and John reporting that they're going to be tied up at the Conwy facility for a few more days."

Diane nodded. "I filed the paperwork earlier. How are the kids doing?"

"They're doing well. Craig still has both hands, believe it or not."

"I'll bet he doesn't make it to the end of the term without some sort of injury. Those Wechselbalg kids think they're invincible from the moment the hormones hit them."

Dorene raised an eyebrow in interest. "I'll take that bet. What are the stakes?"

"How about *steaks*? Loser buys the other dinner for a month."

Dorene grinned. "Sounds good to me. I'll enjoy all that free food."

Diane shook her head, her nose wrinkled. "Don't count on it, DJ. I don't think he's learned his lesson yet. I had a talk with his father after the moon incident, and even *he* doesn't think Craig's going to make it through unscathed."

"Did you share our concerns about safety?"

"I did, and the response was along the lines of 'he's just like I was at that age, he'll grow out of it.'" Diane groaned. "I'm just wondering how many body parts he's going to lose before that happens—or if they'll all be his own." She tsked her disapproval. "You know as well as I do that he's as likely to endanger someone else as he is himself. You know what puberty does to boys—they're all squeaky voices and impulse. We can't have that happen. One wrong move up here, and *BANG!* We're all floating in the vacuum of space with our eyes popping out of our skulls."

Dorene shook her head to remove the thoughts of Craig setting off a chain reaction that destroyed them all. "I think you're worrying too much. He has John and Jean watching over him. Do you think they'd let him mess around?"

Diane shrugged. Student welfare was her sister's realm. "If you say so. What about Cheryl Lynn's group? How are they doing?"

Dorene looked down at her notes. "Jayden is a born organizer, Cheryl Lynn says. Yana is still timid, but getting more confident by the day. Cheryl Lynn says she will do well in a diplomatic position when she's older, unless she chooses to pursue a humanitarian role."

Diane agreed. "Perhaps she'll take over for us, when we retire. Again."

They cackled like a pair of witches over steaming mugs in place of bubbling cauldrons.

"We're not going to talk about that retirement nonsense again, are we, DJ?" Diane eventually said. "I mean, a vacation now and then would be nice, but I kind of like it here." She looked out the open door into the dim lobby, where the glow of the galaxy on the ceiling was the only source of light.

"We're not even going to make it out of this office if we don't get a move on," Dorene said, putting her empty mug down and picking her tablet up again. "Where were we?"

Diane was already there. "Cheryl Lynn's group, DJ. Just Ksenia to discuss. She recommends a diplomatic role for her as well. Do we have a track in place for that?"

"We can put one in place. Build it up from the negotiations class with Ecaterina. Who would be the best person for that?"

"I suspect Anna Elizabeth Hauser, but I may be wrong. I'll ask Cheryl Lynn in the morning. The General—how are his future officers shaping up?"

"You mean the Echo and Foxtrot snowflakes? Decidedly less snowflakey after a few weeks with him, I'm glad to say. Deciding to send them as a group to Lance was a good idea. Maybe next term their mentor won't have so much trouble with them."

"*All* the mentors are reporting that they're having success with their assigned students." Diane high-fived her sister. "In fact, I would say our experiment is a resounding success!"

"Shall we get out of here?" Dorene asked with a glint in her eye. "I feel some late-night shopping coming on."

Diane already had her bag in her hand and was halfway to the door. "You don't have to ask me twice!"

United Kingdom, North Wales, Snowdonia National Park, Caernarvon, Llyn Cwm Ffynnon

Broadbent squinted as the reflection of the sun off the lake momentarily blinded him. His radio spat out Perkins' garbled voice, interspaced with hissed bursts of static.

"Sir? I can't hear you, sir."

"Speak up, Perkins, the signal is terrible here." Broadbent hit the receiver against his leg a couple of times and tried again. This time he could hear Perkins loud and clear.

"It's the mountains, sir. I have a location for John Grimes. HQ says you're to get eyes on him, and report his activities back to them ASAP."

"He's got five kids with him. It's not like he's going to be plotting to overthrow the government. Can't they just send the satellite over? They're most likely out here for camping, or some other banal outdoorsy activity."

"It won't be in position for another three hours, sir. Besides, every time we try to get a lock on them the satellite goes on the fritz. It's bloody eerie."

Broadbent sighed, rubbing his face with his free hand.

Damn this assignment! If it wasn't super-powered TQB employees making his day unbearable, it was HQ with yet another set of orders that violated his personal code. That in itself wouldn't be too much, but dealing with Captain Myerscough was a battle all its own.

Maybe he should have married Susan all those years ago. Settled down and had a family, instead of running off to play out his childhood *James Bond* fantasies.

"Sir, you're sighing a lot lately. Is everything all right?"

"Fine, Perkins. I'll be in touch shortly."

"Very good, sir." Perkins signed off.

Broadbent approached Myerscough's tent with a heaviness in his step. He nodded to the guards, who relaxed their weapons when they saw it was him.

"Afternoon, lads. Is he inside?"

The guard on the left nodded. "Yes, sir, but he's not himself, today, sir. Tread lightly."

Broadbent held his sigh in. Perkins was right—he *was* sighing a lot recently. He told himself that after this assignment he was going to retire. He'd been thinking about it since his fortieth birthday had come and gone, but whereas it had always been a joke between him and Perkins before, being made to risk his life for the sake of traipsing around Snowdonia to spy on a bunch of kids was making the idea of a cottage by the sea look more attractive by the minute.

He entered the tent, calling, "Only me, Captain. May I come in?"

Myerscough sat behind the desk in the middle of the tent while his secretaries bustled in the background. Broadbent saw mess everywhere. Myerscough looked up at Broadbent with red-rimmed eyes. Had the man even slept? He looked like he was having a breakdown.

"Ah, Broadbent. Good to see you, old chap. Did you hear from HQ? Did they say we can leave?" He looked up hopefully at Broadbent. The secretaries beat a hasty retreat from the tent while Myerscough wasn't paying attention.

That told Broadbent everything. He'd seen this kind of thing a lot in recent times: officers who had previously had a sterling record losing their courage at the thought of facing TQB. He was glad the guard had warned him of Myerscough's condition. He could get things done faster if he wasn't butting heads with the army fellows.

He shook his head. "Not quite, Captain. I'm to get eyes-on and report back."

"Better you than me," Myerscough mumbled.

Broadbent made a face to show his displeasure. "Did all the patrols come back in yet? I'd like to sit in on the debrief, if you don't mind."

The captain frowned. "Patrols? Oh yes, of course, Agent."

Broadbent was more than concerned. Myerscough seemed to be losing his grip, not ideal when a single mistake could bring the full fury of TQB down upon them. "Captain, is there anything I can do for you? You need to pull it together, sir. Your men are depending on you."

"How the hell am I supposed to do that?" Myerscough spluttered. "Have you *seen* what one of those Bitches is capable of? We're as good as dead if we carry on interfering, man. I say we avoid kicking the hornet's nest."

Broadbent was aghast. "*Captain!* Get hold of yourself! The men are just outside. What if they hear you talking like this? You have a sworn duty, and I didn't peg you for a coward."

This made Myerscough's hackles rise and he stood up, leaning against the desk for support. His face reddened and he hesitated a couple of times before he found the words to speak. When he did, his voice was deathly quiet and steady.

"Coward? I am not a coward, sir, and how dare you accuse me of such a thing! I was fighting in wars while you were still getting your botty changed by your mummy, so don't talk to *me* about courage!" He slammed a meaty fist on the desk, causing his drink to spill over the edge of the tin mug he was using.

His mustache bristled with indignation as he launched into a full-on rant, just as Broadbent intended. They were too easy, these army types.

"I have dodged bullets, outrun missiles, and fought hand-to-hand with insurgents hell-bent on destroying our way of life. I'll not be spoken to like this by you! Damn spook, what do you know? I've *seen* John Grimes in action, and I'm not talking about the videos of him slicing through hordes of monsters like they were butter. I was *there*...in the desert..." He wiped the sweat from his top lip. "Agent, I am not afraid for myself, but for my men. What will he do when he finds out we've been watching them? These boys have *families*!"

Broadbent nodded sympathetically. "Just so, sir. I'm no happier than you about this, but orders are orders, and there's more at stake here. I'll be joining the debrief, then I need a couple of men for an observation."

Myerscough was lost in his memories again.

"I'll see myself out, sir," Broadbent murmured, backing out of the tent.

He paused by the guards. "What are your names, soldiers?"

"The name's Barrowclough, sir," the younger one said.

"Eggy, sir," was all the older soldier said, not taking his focus from his duty for a second.

Broadbent liked the older soldier's circumspect manner. Barrowclough wasn't seasoned enough to have a nickname yet. Eggy would have the information Broadbent needed.

"Good to meet you, Eggy. Walk with me, if you will."

Eggy was experienced enough to understand that Broadbent's request was rhetorical. He fell in behind Broadbent as the agent strolled away from the tent.

They walked in silence for a short way until Broadbent deemed they were out of the captain's hearing, coming to rest at a boulder near the edge of camp.

He took out a packet of cigarettes and offered one to Eggy. Nothing was more predictable than a hardened soldier. His guess was right, because the soldier took one, lit it, and blew a cloud of stinking smoke all around.

Broadbent had an in. He lit a cigarette of his own, trying not to gag on the taste. He wasn't a smoker, but whatever got the job done. He needed this soldier at ease for his questions.

He scuffed the ground with his boot. "I have to ask, Eggy—is the Captain always this high-strung?"

The squaddie shook his head. "I've been with him fifteen years," he said sadly. "I've never seen him like this. The lads are worried, sir, if you don't mind me speaking freely."

Broadbent nodded. "Speak freely, Eggy. Goodness knows there's little opportunity to do so."

"It's John Grimes, sir. We've seen the Bitches before, you see." Eggy looked distant.

"Yes, Myerscough did say something about the desert."

Eggy nodded. "We were in the dustbowl with the Americans when it happened. They came out of nowhere and destroyed a refinery. None of our telemetry picked up their ships. They were in and out before we could do a thing, sir. Blood *everywhere*."

"Civilians?" Broadbent was horrified.

"Oh *lord*, no!" Eggy's expression was almost one of hero worship. "They were ISIS scumbags, sir. Not one person died who didn't deserve it. That op made me consider going AWOL, if I'm honest, sir. We'd been out there for weeks, watching the terrorists and waiting for a green light to clear the cockroaches out, and along they came and fixed the problem in just a few minutes. We rounded up the civilians afterwards. They were terrified. They saved them all, sir. It don't sit right with me at all that we're working secretly against them." He realized what he'd said and shut his mouth.

Broadbent reassured him. "It's all right, Eggy. I'm in agreement with you, but as I've been saying a hell of a lot recently, orders are orders. Hey, what did you see when you went in afterwards? And don't tell me you didn't." Broadbent could tell Eggy was about to clam up again. "I know you all got sent in to poke about for dropped tech. It's been an addendum to protocol on every interaction with TQB recently."

Eggy stared past him at nothing.

"That bad, eh?" Broadbent sympathized.

"They had been annihilated. One looked like someone had ripped his arm off and beat him to death with the soggy end. A whole bunch of them looked like they'd been attacked by an animal. Something had torn them apart like ragdolls."

"I say! Good lord," Broadbent managed.

"That's not even the worst bit." Eggy's eyes were far away, his mouth puckered in distaste. "As we were leaving, one of the guys slipped. It was dark by then, the only light coming from the burning refinery. When we got back in the transport and the lights came on we all saw he was covered in people purée. Never been able to eat marinara since."

Broadbent felt nauseous. He'd seen the reports from around the world on that night. "Did you see any of it happen?"

Eggy shook his head, crushing the butt of his cigarette under the heel of his boot. "No, sir. They obliterated them so fast we only truly saw it on the surveillance footage afterwards. We wouldn't have even had *that* if our main cam unit hadn't broken down the week before. We were using an old camcorder we picked up in the market, along with our issued surveillance package, and that was the only thing that wasn't wiped when we got back. The captain is just worried that will happen to us. He's a good man, sir. He'll pull through."

Broadbent patted the soldier's shoulder. "I'll see what I can do to get him some help. In the meantime, who would you choose if you needed a sneaky recce done?"

"Bright and Hobson without a doubt, sir. Them lads are more like ninjas than soldiers. You'll find them in the mess tent, prob'ly next to the keg."

Broadbent thanked him. "You're lucky boys, getting a keg laid on for you."

"Oh no, sir. That's due to Captain Myerscough. He has

one shipped in whenever we stay still for more than five minutes."

"I wish my CO was as thoughtful," Broadbent grumbled amicably.

An hour later he crouched atop a ridge on the low peak that would give them an unobstructed view of the valleys below for miles around. Bright had gone ahead to set up their meager equipment. They were keeping watch on the famous Pen Y Gwryd hotel, where the Range Rover carrying their targets had parked forty minutes before.

"Movement ahead, sir," Sergeant Bright said in a voice too low to carry and give their position away. "It appears they're leaving."

Broadbent took the digital field glasses Bright proffered, adjusting the zoom and focusing on the vehicle.

"I stayed there once, back in the eighties. Nice place." He watched the car pull away and take the turn leading further west. "I think they're headed for Snowdon."

Bright nodded. "I'd have to agree, sir."

Their suspicions were confirmed a short time later when the vehicle stopped at the Snowdon view point on the road opposite the mountain.

"Is it true that John Grimes can kill you with laser beams from his eyes?" Hobson asked.

Broadbent snorted. "What? No, Hobson! He's as human as the rest of us."

"That's not what I've heard." Hobson looked at Bright, who shook his head. "I heard they're up there getting all pally with the aliens. How do we know they haven't been bodysnatched and the aliens aren't using them to stage a quiet invasion, eh?"

"Shut up, you gormless nitwit," Bright snapped. "That's just hearsay and rubbish. I don't believe there's any aliens at all. They've got a supercomputer and a hell of a lot of money—*that's* how they're doing all this."

Broadbent ignored the bickering soldiers and continued watching as John Grimes and the children piled out of the car. The kids stood at the railing looking at the mountain while Grimes pulled a few hefty-looking rucksacks out of the boot and dumped them on one of the picnic tables. He pulled a device from his pocket and started to talk.

"I wish we had audio," Broadbent muttered.

Hobson stepped forwards. "I can lip-read, sir."

"Why are you only telling me this now?" He passed Hobson the field glasses. "Well, what are they saying?"

"Hang on a minute, sir. The zoom's acting up." Hobson fiddled with the buttons on the side to adjust the zoom. A second later he threw the field glasses to the ground with a yelp as they released a puff of acrid smoke. "They burned me!"

Broadbent peered at the place they'd landed. The grass they had landed on was turning brown as the field glasses warped from the heat they were producing. The casing burst with a pop, startling the three of them.

"*Poxy bloody technology!*" Broadbent swore. "We'd better move to a closer vantage point before they leave the view point and we lose them."

United Kingdom, North Wales, Conwy Castle, Manufacturing Floor, Store Room

Tina giggled as Ron nuzzled her nose with his. She tucked her hair behind her ear with one hand and pushed him away gently with the other. "Come on, we'd better get back with these packing materials before Ms. Dukes notices we've been gone too long."

They were helping break down the equipment that was scheduled to be shipped to the *Meredith Reynolds* later in the week. Jean had sent them to the store room almost fifteen minutes ago.

Ron stood with a glazed look in his eyes. She thumped his arm, giggling again at the effect she'd had on him. "Earth to Ron! The boxes!"

He jerked back to reality, blushing brightly. "Um, sure thing."

His fumbling attempt to pull the stack of flat-packed boxes from the shelf was a failure. His grip slipped and he stumbled backwards, banging his head on the shelf behind.

Tina winced at the solid *thunk* his skull made as it connected.

Ron crumpled to the floor, holding his head. "*Oooww!*"

Tina had just bent down to see what damage he'd done when the door opened and Jean came in. "What are you two up to?"

"It's Ron, Ms. Dukes. He's banged his head," Tina explained. She saw no sense in telling their teacher *why* it had happened.

Jean crossed the narrow room and knelt beside him. "Let me see, Ron."

Ron moaned and took his hand off the egg forming on the back of his head. "Please don't let Doctor Llewellyn get me, Ms. Dukes. I'll be a good boy, I promise!" His eyes swam, unfocused. A moment later Jean and Tina narrowly avoided being spattered by vomit as he threw up.

"Looks like he's got a concussion, I'm going to take him to the infirmary," Jean said, frowning in concern. She scooped him up as though he weighed nothing and carefully carried him out of the storage area. "Come on, Tina. You can sit with him and keep him awake while he recovers. I think we both know why he wasn't paying attention."

She hurried toward the elevators, Tina scurrying to keep up.

The matron confirmed Ron's concussion and admitted him to the infirmary for observation. He had begun to talk normally after the matron gave him some fluids to replace what he'd lost when he'd been sick, and the matron had said he could sleep once she was satisfied the concussion was not severe.

Tina sat by his bed watching him sleep as the IV line fed him a mixture of ibuprofen, paracetamol, and fluids to reduce the risk of swelling and help with his pain. She'd asked for an explanation of everything as the matron calmly bustled about taking care of Ron earlier, and the short version was that he would be fine after some rest.

The infirmary was too quiet. Tina got her tablet out and opened the Bootstrapping app, thinking she'd pass the time that way. Aleksi's version was still available from the previous session, so she selected it from the menu and began a new game with the same parameters.

One of the nice things about dating a fellow superbrain was that she and Ron spent hours talking about everything they loved to geek out about. He had told her all about the history of the castle, how it was one of a ring of castles that had been built around Snowdonia by the English king back in the twelve hundreds to oppress the Welsh.

The renovation teams had made the castle into a fortress once more, ensuring that only TQB employees could reach the facility. The only remaining vulnerabilities were from air or sea attacks.

The game was ready, and Tina began preparing her inventory for the impending attack. The first time she'd played the game, the enemy had come overland using tanks. The Challenger IIs had halted on the opposite bank of the River Conwy and fired on the walls using high-explosive squash-head rounds designed for penetrating stonework, then opened up with their chain-guns when the HESH rounds had breached the walls. They had lost that game by a mile after the army and navy moved in.

This time Tina would be ready for them. She had been helping Jean disassemble and pack the manufacturing and production lines, so she now had a better idea of what was available in the castle inventory—and also where she would find the ideal components to be repurposed into her defenses.

Half an hour later she was putting the finishing touches to her setup when Ron stirred, waking up. She paused the game and got up to get him a glass of water.

She held the glass out, and he smiled sheepishly as he accepted it. "Hey," he said awkwardly. "It's a dangerous thing, falling for a beautiful woman like you."

Tina blushed at the compliment. "Stop being so cheesy, Ron! How are you feeling?"

He sipped the water and caught one of the ice-chips in his mouth before setting the glass down on the over-bed table. "I've been better. What did the matron say after I fell asleep?"

"That you'll be fine after you rest." She bit her lip, carefully reaching out to take his hand so she didn't disturb the canula taped to the back of it. "Geez, Ron. You scared the crap out of me, talking nonsense all the way from the storeroom to the infirmary. When you brought up you-know-who I thought you were going to tell Ms. Dukes *everything!*"

Ron's dark-ringed eyes looked blank. "Huh?"

"You know, the doctor," she whispered, looking at the door to Ron's room, which was ajar.

"Oh, yeah." Ron yawned.

She stroked his head. "You should get back to sleep. Rest and get better, so we can get you out of here."

He had already closed his eyes. She pulled the crisp sheet up around his ears and went back to her game.

CHAPTER TWELVE

United Kingdom, North Wales, Snowdonia, Llyn Gwynant

John led the students into the forest. He ignored the campsite completely, piquing Maxim's curiosity. The low sun threw diamonds onto the lake and the lapping waves scattered them as the birds wheeled above the water, catching his eye as he speculated on why they were heading away from the regular humans and out into the wilderness.

"Turn down your thoughts," John said quietly from ahead. "Reach out with your senses. What can you hear? What can you smell?"

Maxim did as he was told, breathing deeply through his nose. "Cows and sheep?"

Craig let rip with a rumbling fart. "I smell cheese!" He guffawed.

"Ew, Craig. Gross!" Masha complained.

"Yeah, dude, gross!" Halli gagged, her extra-keen Wechselbalg senses overwhelmed.

John laughed and forged ahead through the trees, creating a path through the undergrowth. "Focus on what you can hear. Start with your immediate surroundings, and work your way out. Try to guess what *I* can hear. I'll give you one clue…it's alive, and it's *small*. Whoever gets it right gets first choice on the food substitutes tonight."

Maxim listened carefully. He heard his own heartbeat, and the heartbeats of the others. He heard his teammates breathing, and the rumble of someone's stomach.

"I think I'd rather catch a rabbit," he heard Craig mutter under his breath.

He extended his focus past the group, slowing his breathing so he could hear better. He was confused as he scanned the area, but his sense of smell confirmed his findings —anything that had been near them had made itself scarce.

"What are you hearing, sir?" he asked. "There are no animals or birds in the area around us."

John gave a small rueful smile. "An unfortunate side-effect of being such a badass—I mean, having *my* level of enhancement—is that I tend to scare the smarter animals away just by being there. You kids have the same effect, just less intense because you're not fully grown yet. Any of you ever tried to pet a cat?"

They all nodded.

"Cats hate us, sir," Halli admitted.

"That's to be expected, since you smell like wolves. Now that we've established there's nothing in the immediate vicinity, widen your search."

The students obeyed, sniffing the air deeply.

Maxim smelled people, but not nearby. It was a slightly

sour scent, as though they hadn't washed for a few days. Campers, he thought. He was distracted from his musings by Craig's victory whoop.

"A...a... A *something*! That way!" Craig pointed off into the trees. "I hear its heart!"

"Very good, Craig. You get dessert too if you can tell me what it is."

Craig screwed up his face as he tried to pin down the scent. Maxim and the others put similar effort into pinpointing what Craig had found.

"It is a rodent, I know that much," Maxim offered. He even knew what kind of rodent it was, but it was good for Craig to get a chance to shine.

"Is it a mouse?" Craig asked.

"Looks like we have a winner for round one!" John cheered. "Keep going. Next person gets to pick their camp duty for tonight..."

They all enjoyed the game, 'finding' a rabbit burrow, numerous bird's nests, and a beehive—along with a number of rodents and other small forest creatures as they hiked along paths that John created as he walked.

He came to a halt as they entered a small clearing on a gentle slope. "Round two, let's see who can get their tent set up the quickest. The prize is... Hmmm, let's see. First watch. Last one done sits the graveyard watch with me."

"How is guard duty a prize?" Masha complained. "It is work!"

John's face was contemplative. "Until you've done overnight sentry duty, I just can't tell you, Masha. Your classmates have already made a good start on their tents, so if you don't hurry up with yours, you'll see *why* first watch is a prize."

A short time later the clearing had been transformed into a camp for the night.

In the center they had a fire burning merrily, surrounded by stones to keep the forest safe. Maxim took a seat on one of the logs they'd dragged in, joining the others as they accepted the food packs John handed out from one of the backpacks.

"Eat up. You're going to need the calories." John wiggled an eyebrow mysteriously as he gave them all an extra ration.

"Why?" Craig inquired through a mouthful of hot stroganoff.

John grinned. "Did any of you sense anything besides the animals?"

Maxim thought about it for a moment, trying to work out what John wanted them to have smelled. "People," he said simply. "It was faint, but it's been there all day. I assumed it was hikers, like us."

"Me too!" Mischa cried. The others nodded and agreed that they'd smelled something here and there.

John pulled five more pouches out of the backpack and tossed them to the students. "Extra dessert for you all. I didn't sense them at all, but I *did* get a call letting me know we were being watched from a distance."

Halli paled. "Are we in danger?"

John pulled a face. "With me? Never. Now, I'm not sure if they have eyes on us now, so after dinner I want the five of you to go into the trees and change."

"You mean *change* change?"

Craig was not alone in his disbelief. The dessert pouches were forgotten as they all began to speak at once.

John held up a hand. "One at a time."

"We are not allowed to do that on the mudball," Maxim informed him when they quieted down.

John chuckled. "I won't tell if you don't."

Halli asked, "What if whoever is watching sees us?"

John's smile widened and Maxim could have sworn he had a twinkle in his eye. "I'm counting on it, Halli. Now get those calories in. I'm waiting on another call, and then we're going for a nice, long run."

United Kingdom, North Wales, Snowdonia

Broadbent and the soldiers were in position on the peak above the camp, watching the activity below using old-fashioned binoculars.

No fancy technology to inexplicably combust this time. He'd made them ditch anything that carried a signal before they relocated to their present spot.

He glanced to his left. "What's going on? What's he saying, Hobson?"

Hobson shrugged uncomfortably. "I dunno, sir. It's getting too dark to see."

Broadbent tutted. "Well, keep watching. I'm going to get a bite to eat." He shuffled backwards until he was clear of the ghillie net they'd slung for a hide and took a packet of rice pudding and a spoon from his pack.

A few bites into his cold dinner, he heard Bright calling him softly.

He rushed back over and picked his binoculars up just

in time to see the kids walk away from the camp in opposite directions.

"What are they doing?" he muttered to no one in particular.

"He's probably sent them for firewood, sir," Bright offered.

Hobson agreed. "Yeah, sir. Look, it's getting low."

The next thing that happened would stay with them forever.

Out of the tree line where the children had entered padded five shaggy wolves. They loped across the clearing back to the camp, where they laid at John Grimes' feet.

The two soldiers made the connection almost immediately and scrambled out of the area, down the opposite side of the peak.

"Where are you going?" Broadbent hissed.

"We need to tell the captain to bring in reinforcements," Bright called over his shoulder.

"No way we can take them on, not just the three of us, if they spot us. It's suicide to stay here. They're not kids, they're *monsters!*" Hobson added.

Broadbent knew all about the Wechselbalg, as they called themselves. The British Government had worked hard to make sure that kind of thing did not become the ordinary citizen's problem.

Now it was his problem.

Broadbent sighed and set off after the retreating soldiers.

CHAPTER THIRTEEN

BBS *Meredith Reynolds*, Konstantinov Quarters

"Do you like it?" Yana watched Bai Hu with a hopeful expression as he saw his room for the first time.

"It is good! *Xièxiè*. My thanks, Yana." His English was improving with every day that passed.

One of the gifts sent by Bethany Anne and her people had been a tablet of his own, with games designed to build his vocabulary. He had a quick mind, she had learned. She hoped he would make it into the Academy when he was old enough to take the test so she could keep an eye on him.

He bowed his head and stood awkwardly by the holowindow Nestor had made for him from an old projector. His expression was wistful as he watched the shifting views of his old home.

"It does not have to show China," Yana said. She picked up a small remote control from the bedside cabinet and flicked through the preprogrammed scenes, pausing on a snowy forest. "See? This is Russia, my homeland. It is beautiful, no?"

"It is," Bai Hu agreed. He ran his hand over the soft bedspread with a troubled expression on his face. "Yana, will I see China again?"

Yana's heart broke for the little werecat. "Oh, *kotenok*, it is not as simple as that. It's too dangerous to go back there." She wrapped a sisterly arm around his shoulders and pulled him into a hug.

He snuffled against her cheek. "What is '*kotenok*'?"

"It is Russian for 'kitten.' Do you not like it?"

"Yes, I like. You are *jiějiě*."

Yana released him and smiled. "What is that?"

Bai Hu searched for the word unsuccessfully. He shrugged, looking up at the ceiling and saying the first name he'd learned upon waking. "Meredith."

Meredith's cool tones came from the speakers. "Yes, Bai Hu? How can I help you?"

At least that was what Yana assumed Meredith said, because the EI was speaking Chinese for Bai Hu's benefit. Bai Hu and Meredith talked back and forth for a minute, then Meredith switched to English to speak to Yana.

"Bai Hu wishes to express his gratitude to you and your father for taking him into your home. The word he used means 'sister,' or more accurately 'elder sister.'"

"*Xièxiè*, Meredith," Bai Hu told the EI.

"Yes, thank you, Meredith," Yana added.

"You are welcome, children. Call again if you need me."

"Goodbye!"

Yana held out a hand to her little brother. "Come, it is

time for me to meet Nestor and talk to my friends down on Earth. I want to tell them all about my little brother!"

"They are down there?" Bai Hu was clearly concerned. "Are they in danger? Like China?"

Yana shook her head. "They are in a safe place. You will see!"

She led him out of the family quarters and along the corridor to the tram station.

When the tram arrived, she guided Bai Hu to an empty car and they kept teaching each other words until they reached the stop for the Etheric Academy. Yana's Mandarin would soon be as good as her English.

Bai Hu stared around. He was amazed by life on the *Meredith Reynolds*. He had taken the news that they were among the stars very well when it was explained to him by her father.

Considering he'd had no experience of anything outside his village before the soldiers came for his family, he was coping well with all the new ideas he'd been introduced to now that he had recovered from his ordeal.

Nestor waited for them at the tram station. He hugged Yana, and held a hand out for Bai Hu to shake. "Heeeey, look who is out of the medical wing!"

"Nestor," Bai Hu said warmly, ignoring the hand and bowing deeply instead. "*Xièxiè*, the gift. It brings me joy."

Nestor grinned, stowing his hand and bowing in return. "It was my pleasure. Let us get to the dorm. They will be calling us soon."

They stopped for a moment when they passed through the doors and Bai Hu saw the main lobby for the first time.

He let out a sigh of wonder when he saw the stars dance across the ceiling. *"Tā tài piàoliangle!* The stars!"

"I know that one, it means 'it's so pretty'. He says it a lot," Yana told Nestor with a smile.

Bai Hu did a slow circle underneath the galaxy on the ceiling with an expression of pure joy on his face. His rotation stalled suddenly and he pointed up. *"Jiějiě,* it changes!"

Yana and Nestor looked up to where Bai Hu pointed. The ever-shifting representation of the galaxy twinkled above their heads.

Bai Hu pointed again. "There!"

They all saw the star system wink into existence where there had been a relatively empty space before.

Nestor's eyes shone. "Meredith, are you there?"

"Always," Meredith answered instantly. "Good evening, Nestor. How may I help you?"

"We just saw a new star system appear on the galaxy model. Why is that?" Nestor didn't take his eyes off the ceiling.

"The model is continually updated to reflect our expanding knowledge of the stars," Meredith replied.

"Good to know," Yana said to Meredith, then, "We have to go. It's time to call the team."

"Thank you, Meredith," Nestor said. "Goodnight!"

"Farewell, children."

They raced up the right-hand staircase, arriving in the Alpha Class dormitory as Nestor's tablet began to buzz.

"Just give me a second." He plugged his tablet into the TV monitor in the common area and accepted the call.

Tina, Ron, and Aleksi appeared on the screen. Yana was

concerned to see that Ron looked tired and pale. They all appeared troubled.

"What is wrong?" she asked. "Is everything okay down there?"

Tina shook her head somberly. "No, not really."

United Kingdom, North Wales, Conwy Castle, Student Dormitory

Earlier that day...

Tina dried her hair with a towel, tied it back out of the way, and pulled her coverall on over her sweats in preparation for going back to work.

Ron was sleeping soundly, so she headed for the packing bay. She wasn't the type of person to leave it to others when there was a job to be done.

She thought about the smartphone while she made her way down the stairs to the manufacturing floor. Logically, it must belong to whoever was running Doctor Llewellyn.

She left her ruminations behind as she pushed the plastic curtain aside to enter the bay she'd been working in before Ron's accident.

The breakdown was in full swing, and moving rapidly toward completion. She saw that much of the machinery which had been there when they arrived was gone. The rest was in the process of being disassembled by the facility's staff and Jean's techs, ready to be packed and taken to Jean's R&D labs on the *Meredith Reynolds*. The buzz of the adults' conversation added another layer to the chorus of clangs, bangs, and power tools.

Jean noticed Tina and waved her over to a bay at the far

end of the floor, where she found Aleksi stripping what remained of a robotic arm. He was focused on the task, so she waited until he'd removed the piece he was working on and turned to put it on the cart beside his bench.

Aleksi looked up, putting his tools down when he saw her. "Hey! How is Ron?" he asked, speaking loudly to be heard over the commotion.

"It was a mild concussion. He'll be back at the dorm by tonight, just in time for our call home," she replied. "It's a shame Maxim is off in the forest with John. He'll be sad to miss a chance to talk to Nestor if they don't get back in time."

"They'll be back together as soon as all this work is done and we can go home." He held a socket wrench out to Tina.

She took it with a grin. "True. What are we doing this afternoon?"

Aleksi smiled ruefully. "More of the same. Strip whatever we're given down to its constituent parts, fill the cart, and take it to Jean and Doctor Llewellyn to be either packed and sent up or taken to the furnaces to be smelted and *then* sent up."

Tina took another of the robotic arms from the pile of mismatched parts waiting to be disassembled and settled down next to Aleksi at the bench. The time passed quickly, the rhythm created by the adults working guiding their pace as they reduced the pile.

When their carts were full they left the bay, pushing them to the edge of the area where the walkway was wide enough for them to walk side-by-side without obstructing anyone walking the other way.

There was a short wait when they got to Jean's station. Doctor Llewellyn was just leaving through the plastic curtain when they got to the front of the queue of people waiting to drop off their carts.

"Where do you think she's going?" Tina asked Aleksi quietly.

Aleksi shook his head. "I do not know. Maybe we should follow her?"

Tina pursed her lips. "How will we get away without being noticed?" A thought occurred to her. "Leave it to me."

They moved forward as the adult in front of them deposited his cart and left with an empty one.

Jean looked up from her station at the workbench, smiling brightly at Tina and Aleksi when she saw them pushing their carts over to her assistant. "Hey, I wasn't expecting you to finish so soon! Great job, kids."

"Thank you, Ms. Dukes," Aleksi said.

"Would it be okay if we stretched our legs before starting the next batch?" Tina asked hopefully.

Jean was distracted by the parts scattered around her station. "Huh? Oh, yeah, sure. Just don't go into any of the restricted areas." She already had her head down again and was focused on her work.

"We'll go and visit Ron," Tina told her.

They said goodbye, receiving a distracted grunt and a wave in return, and left the floor in the same direction Doctor Llewellyn had exited a few minutes before.

"Where do you think she went?" Aleksi asked when they were in the corridor. They dismissed the elevator, which was still sat waiting on their level, headed past the sign at the nexus of corridors directing employees to the different workspaces, and went through the stairwell door.

Tina looked up through the middle of the windowless stairwell, trying to guess. "I don't know." She saw the flicker of a lab coat two stories up, which was ground-level.

Shortly thereafter they heard a door close.

"She's on the ground floor," Tina said. "She's probably headed for her office. Come on!" She ran up the stairs, treading softly to avoid the echo.

Aleksi panted as he kept pace behind her. "What are we going to do when we find her? If we get caught snooping around near her office again, she'll *know* we had something to do with the phone going missing."

Tina halted at the door leading into the main hall on the ground floor. "It's in the same building as the infirmary, which is why I told Ms. Dukes we were going there. What do you think we should do?"

"We should keep moving, at least," Aleksi said after a moment. "We can make a decision when we get to the main hall. Is there anyone out there now?"

Tina pushed the door open a crack and peered into the hall. "Not that I can see." She went into the hall, Aleksi following close behind.

"Don't skulk. It makes you look guilty," she told him. "Just walk normally, like you're supposed to be here. Haven't you ever broken the rules before?"

Aleksi straightened up. "Have *you* broken them often?"

"Not as often as you think," she retorted with a wink. "That's better. Come on, we'll take the front way. Then if anyone asks, we say we're going to see Ron in the infirmary."

They crossed the hall, heading for the corridor that led to the old visitor's center, which now housed the infirmary and administration offices.

Tina shuddered at the change in temperature between the hall and the windowless corridor. She was about to complain when the lights went out, plunging them into darkness.

They immediately turned and went back through the door to the hall, where the stained-glass windows let in the late afternoon sun.

"Sabotage!" they exclaimed in unison.

Tina's heart beat faster. "She must have gone to the generator room and cut the power. But why?"

Aleksi had the answer. "To cause a distraction. That's what I'd do. Get everyone in one place so I could be in another."

Just then their tablets began to bleep.

Tina was almost relieved. "It's Ms. Dukes, so we'd better answer."

Jean's face appeared. There was a line in the middle of her forehead that told them not to say anything that would inconvenience her further. "Where are you kids?"

"We're in the main hall, Ms. Dukes," Aleksi said.

"Do you want us back on the floor?" Tina added.

Jean shook her head. "No, there's a problem with the power. Work is on hold until it's back up and we have light to see by. You two can take some time; go up to your dorm and stay there until John gets back with the others. I'll be up as soon as I can. We'll all have dinner together tonight."

Tina smiled. "That sounds great. Are you sure we can't help?"

Aleksi made a face where Jean couldn't see. Tina waited nervously to hear Jean's reply.

"No, we're good. You kids go have some leisure time."

Almost clear, Tina thought. "Is John due back soon?"

"Within the next hour or two," Jean confirmed before signing off.

"So, what do we do?" Aleksi asked. "Should we look for Doctor Llewellyn, or go to the dorm?"

Tina gave a shrug. "We may as well go to the dorm. Whatever she needed a distraction for, it worked. I say we look at the phone."

Aleksi's eyebrows shot up. "Are you joking? After everything you said to stop me from looking at it the other night?"

Tina smirked and moved toward the tower door. "Let's just go and get the phone. I have a solution."

The stairway was illuminated only by thin lances of sunlight let in by embrasures farther up. They headed upstairs, activating the torch function on Aleksi's tablet to light the dim spiral as they ascended to the dormitories on the top level.

They walked in silence, concentrating on not falling on the uneven stone steps in the near-dark, but suddenly the silence was broken by a deep scraping sound which echoed around the tower walls. Tina ran toward the sound, rounding the final bend just in time to see the fireplace across the hallway grinding shut.

"What the hell?" Aleksi said from behind her.

Tina let out a small scream and spun without thinking, taking a swing at Aleksi.

Aleksi backpedaled and held his hands up, dazzling her with the light from his tablet. "Easy there! You almost got me!"

"Oh, it's just you!" Tina almost hugged him in her relief. "Sorry, Aleksi."

Aleksi had already forgotten about it. He went to the fireplace and used his free hand to feel around the edges, since they'd seen the fireplace move. "It is a secret passage, Tina—like Ron told us about!"

She joined him, closely inspecting the crevasse between the wall and the fireplace. "I can't even tell. If I hadn't seen it, I would never have guessed it was a secret door. I wonder who was up here?"

He stepped back and looked at the wall as a whole. "It's seamless. I can't see a way in. It must have been Doctor Llewellyn."

"That's not good." Tina bit her lip. "Do you think she was looking for the phone?"

Aleksi's eyes widened in the dark. "What if she found it?"

They gasped in unison and rushed into the dormitory, where they made a beeline for the sleeping area. Light from the windows helped them avoid falling over the furniture as they tore over to the bunks.

They scrambled underneath Maxim and Craig's bunk and pulled out the loose stone they'd hidden the phone behind.

"Whew!" Aleksi grabbed both items and Tina put the stone back in place.

They wriggled out from under the bunk and dusted themselves down.

"What next?" Aleksi asked. "You didn't tell me your plan."

Tina raised a knowing eyebrow. "Did you stop to read the sign on the wall downstairs?"

Aleksi admitted that he hadn't.

"Well, *I* did," Tina said, grinning smugly. "There's a Faraday room down there." She went over to her bunk and pulled a dark knit cap from the drawers.

Aleksi drew a blank. "A *what* room?"

"A Faraday room," she repeated. "Like a Faraday cage, but bigger. The facility has a whole *room* capable of blocking signals."

Aleksi turned and headed for the door. "What are we waiting for? Let's go!"

Tina stopped him before he got ahead of himself. "It's no good to us until the power is fixed."

He visibly deflated, and slumped into a chair.

Tina grabbed Aleksi's backpack and patted him on the shoulder. "Ms. Dukes will have it back on soon. Here's your bag of gadgets. We'll go see if Ron's ok."

United Kingdom, North Wales, Conwy Castle, Infirmary

Matron smiled warmly at Tina as she entered the infirmary with Aleksi in tow. "Hello, Tina. Nice to see you again, my dearie." She looked Aleksi up and down, smiling warmly. "You must be Aleksandr. I recognize you from the photo in your medical file."

Aleksi shook his head. "Just Aleksi, please, Matron. Only my father calls me Aleksandr."

"Is it okay if we see Ron, Matron?" Tina asked, returning the smile. She liked the motherly woman.

"I can do better than that," Matron said, coming out from behind her desk. "You can take him back to the dorm with you, if you like. He's clear to go, as long as he's supervised. I was about to take young Ronald back to the dormitory before the power cut, but now I must transfer all the perishable medicines, like Doctor Jiani's insulin, to the backup refrigeration unit. You'd be doing me a favor."

Tina hid her delight at the stroke of luck. "We can take care of him, Matron."

Ron was dressed and ready to go when they got to his room, and he jumped up from his seat on the edge of the bed when they came in. "Can I go?" He saw Tina and grinned.

Matron pulled a sheet of paper off the clipboard in her hand, giving it to Tina. "Read through this. If he starts having any of these symptoms bring him straight back, do you hear?"

Tina looked over the information. "Yes, ma'am," she said in her most responsible voice.

Matron nodded. "Good. I'd better get back to those medicines. You can see yourselves out."

Tina took Ron's arm as the three of them left the infirmary. "How are you feeling?"

"I feel good," Ron said, stretching his arms out wide. "A little tired from being asleep so long. Why?"

"Not here," Tina said, glancing back at the infirmary to

make sure Matron wasn't in hearing range. "Come on, we need to get going before someone asks what we're doing."

They each took one of Ron's arms, helping him along to preserve his energy. When they reached the main building they took a break to give him a chance to recover.

"Spill," Ron said as they walked. "What's with all the secrecy?"

Aleksi grinned and said softly, "Tina found a way for us to switch the phone on safely."

Ron looked at Tina with awe. "I knew you would," he told her quietly, matching Aleksi's caution. "What's the plan? Does it have anything to do with the power going out?"

They shook their heads at Ron's question.

"The power was Doctor Llewellyn, we're sure," Tina said. "We were following her."

"You were doing *what*?" Ron interrupted.

Tina arched an eyebrow, not appreciating the tone of his voice. "She left in the middle of the shift, so we asked Jean for a break and followed her up to the ground floor. We'd just gone into the corridor leading to the walkway when the power went out."

"There is a secret passage in King's Tower!" Aleksi blurted. "What?" he said to Tina with a shrug. "You were taking too long! *OW!*"

"Serves you right for ruining my story," Tina said, narrowing her eyes in mock rage as she pounded his arm a second time.

Aleksi rubbed his sore arm gingerly. "You don't hit like a girl. Why did you do it again?"

"You have a lot to learn about girls, Aleksi. Now quit

your whining and come on," she ordered, taking Ron's arm again and steering him toward the stairwell. "We have some sneaking around to do."

The power came on when they were halfway down the stairs to the lower levels, causing Ron to swoon at the sudden return of the overhead lights.

Tina caught him. "Ron! Are you all right?" She looked at his eyes, checking for a difference in the size of his pupils as the care instructions Matron had given her said to do. "Your eyes look fine."

He blinked a few times and rubbed his eyes. "So do yours," he said with a wink. "I just went dizzy for a second. I'm all right, scout's honor."

"Were you even *in* the scouts?" she asked skeptically.

"Wouldn't you like to know? Let's go!" He took the railing firmly and descended toward the door at the bottom of the stairs.

Aleksi and Tina shrugged at each other and followed him. "Wait for us," Tina called softly.

When they peered nervously through the little window in the door, the nexus beyond was empty.

"This way," Tina whispered, taking the lead. She took the third corridor to the left of the elevator.

"Where are we going?" Ron asked.

"To the Faraday room, now that the power is back on. I brought this." She gave him a quick flash of the phone in her pocket.

Ron's jaw dropped. "I thought we were going to... Did you say *Faraday* room?" He grinned. "That knock must have scrambled my brains. Perfect! That's exactly what we need! And it's down this way?"

Tina nodded patiently.

Ron was already moving down the empty corridor toward the heavy metal door at the bottom.

He stopped when he saw the red light and the keypad on the door. "How are we supposed to get in? We don't have a keycard."

Aleksi stepped forward, rummaging in his backpack. "This is where I come in." He pulled out a blank keycard with a USB wire attached.

"I am learning more than I want to about people's dark sides on this trip," Ron muttered. He raised a questioning eyebrow, folding his arms.

Aleksi grinned. "Hey, it's no big deal. I can't get the processing power for my games in my quarters, so I made this to get me into somewhere I can. The EI knows all about it, I promise."

Tina and Ron watched Aleksi insert the USB into his tablet and start up an app before putting the keycard into the slot. He tapped his tablet a few times, and the keypad beeped softly.

A moment later the red light turned green, and the door gave a heavy *clunk*.

"Quickly, get inside," Tina urged, pushing the door open with her shoulder.

The lights and ventilation system kicked in as the door closed, startling them for a moment.

"We're such a bunch of scaredy cats!" Aleksi said with a nervous edge to his voice.

"You would be too if you'd been chased by alien killer robots and shot at by the Americans, the French, the Chinese, *and* the Mongolians," Ron snarked.

The light above the door turned green and Tina took the phone out of her pocket. "Leave it, you two. I'm switching the phone on."

The boys flanked her, craning to see the small screen as it came alive in her hand.

"What should we look at first?" Tina asked once the power-up sequence had finished.

"No password?"

Tina shook her head. "No, Aleksi. That's practically *asking* people to take a look, if you ask me. What do you think, then? Messages?"

The boys agreed, so she opened the message box. She didn't try to hide her disappointment. "It's empty."

"Try the gallery," Ron offered.

Tina came out of the message box and clicked on the gallery. "Oh!" She almost dropped the phone—her initial reaction to the single thumbnail in the folder was so strong. "Poor Doctor Llewellyn!"

"What is it?" Ron took the phone from her and clicked on the image to open it. "Oh my God, it's Doctor Llewellyn's family!" He passed the phone to Aleksi, who was equally disturbed.

"Why are those men holding guns? Those little children are terrified!" he cried, clenching his fists. "We were right, she *is* being coerced!"

Just then, the red light above the door turned green.

"Quick, turn the phone off!" Tina hissed.

Aleksi fumbled the off button as he shoved it into his pocket but it was too late. The door was open. The three looked guiltily at the door as Jean strode in, followed by Doctor Llewellyn.

"What are you doing in here?" she demanded hotly. "I told you to stay in your dorm!" She caught sight of Ron and pointed at him. "*You* definitely shouldn't be here!"

"Sorry, Ms. Dukes," they said sheepishly, heads down.

"Never mind *sorry!*" she bawled. "If it hadn't been for Aleksi using his tablet, I wouldn't have been able to find you! Your locator beacons don't work in here, I thought you'd been kidnapped! I specifically told you all *not* to wander, and you choose to ignore me while we're in the middle of a power outage?"

She glared at them all in disappointment. "I expected better of you all. You especially, Tina. How would I explain it to your uncle if anything had happened to you? Or to Jeff if Ronnie had taken a turn for the worse? I *trusted* you." She glared at the students in turn, letting each of them feel the full weight of her disapproval.

Doctor Llewellyn spoke up. "They're just kids, they are, Jean. Don't be too hard on them, hey?"

Jean gave the doctor a look that made it clear her input was neither needed nor welcome.

Tina felt her face burning, tears of shame pricked at her eyes. "I'm so sorry. I didn't think. We just wanted to see the room." She hated lying to Jean, but she didn't want to give the phone up until they all had a chance to talk about what they'd found.

Jean didn't soften a bit. "Get your things. I'm going to make sure you get to the dorm without any more distractions. As of this minute you're on lockdown. No more wandering around unsupervised." She turned on her heel and marched out of the room.

Doctor Llewellyn gave them a sympathetic look before leaving.

Jean didn't speak another word to them as she escorted them to the tower. There was a Guardian at ease in the hallway when they arrived.

Not wanting to risk Jean's further ire, Tina led the boys into the dormitory.

Jean watched the students head into the dorm, nodding to let the Guardian know she would be with him in a moment.

She paused with her hand on the door, ready to close it. "Kids," she called. "James will be outside all night. He knows you're grounded, so don't pester him."

"Yes, ma'am," they said as she closed the door.

"Why do you think there's a Guardian out there?" Ron asked.

Tina pulled both boys by the sleeves over to the far side of the room. "Keep your voices down; he can hear us. The others will be back soon. What time is it?"

Aleksi looked at his tablet. "Almost six, why?"

She plugged her tablet into the TV monitor. "It's time to call Yana and Nestor. You should join us, this concerns us all."

CHAPTER FOURTEEN

United Kingdom, North Wales, Snowdonia, SAS Camp

Broadbent yawned. The night had been long and tense as John Grimes ringed the camp with the kids in their wolf forms. They had never come within sight of the night watch, but the sporadic howls had left them all on edge. He himself wasn't bothered by the TQB kids, but the men were afraid of the Wechselbalg. They had finally ceased their intimidation just before dawn, just when it was too late for any of them to get any rest. It provoked Broadbent no end, they would be cozy up at the castle while he and the SAS lads were left bleary-eyed. He was determined to see a resolution to this pig's breakfast – sooner rather than later.

He paced back and forth across the tent with the phone to his ear. His orders were changing yet again, and he had a burning sensation creeping upwards from his stomach. He listened as the voice went on.

"They've switched the phone on, Broadbent. We have an opportunity to draw that gorilla Grimes out."

"What do you mean, draw him out?" Broadbent's brow furrowed in confusion. "I thought the whole point was to avoid poking the bear, so to speak."

The reply was almost a sneer. "Are you stupid, man? We can't let a chance like this pass! You would do well to remember what happens to operatives who refuse to obey orders, Broadbent. If I tell you to lick my boots, then you'd jolly well better start acclimatizing yourself to the taste of rubber, you chundering nitwit! I had Perkins send another photograph of the family to the mobile device the little rotters stole from the asset's office. As soon as Grimes leaves, you swoop in."

Broadbent winced. He was quite used to the temper tantrums of the higher-ups; usually empty threats from blustering fools with no power whatsoever. He would normally ignore it and achieve the desired ends his own way. He only reacted this time because the threat had the weight of the entire branch behind it.

"Director General," he began. "You know me. I have never been one to hesitate, not even in Kosovo—and we all know what a shambles *that* turned out to be." He remembered the screams from the mortared school building, courtesy of one side's malfunctioning guidance system, and shook the memory from his mind.

"What are you getting at?"

"That's what I was calling in to report, sir. At least five of the TQB children are Wechselbalg. Even when John Grimes leaves, there will still be a minimum of *five* Wechselbalg in the castle. If the young are there, they haven't been left unguarded. We can expect at least two more trained adult Wechselbalg, sir."

The Director General's voice dripped sarcasm. "They're not even human, Broadbent. If they get in your way, see to it that there are none left to get between you and Jean Dukes' guns. I'll send more men and some additional ordnance, if it will make you happy."

Broadbent sighed, knowing full well that it had more to do with greed. Laura Llewellyn had reported that the Dukes' weapon was stored in a safe in Jean's suite at the top of the King's Tower during the day. The children were bunked in the suite next door. "They're just kids, sir. Is there no other way?"

"We've spent too long doing this the nice way. Stop being such a pathetic lily-livered wet blanket and get on with it, Broadbent! I don't care if you have to end every life in that damned castle—*do your duty!*"

The line went dead before he could acquiesce.

Broadbent took a minute to compose himself. When he'd called to check in with Perkins, he'd been transferred to the DG before he had a chance to brief Perkins of the discovery he'd made in the forest. Perhaps there was still time to avert the disaster. He couldn't live with the deaths of any more children on his conscience. Even if they *were* the children of monsters.

He dialed again, tapping a foot as he waited for Perkins to pick up.

"Sir?"

He was almost relieved to hear the analyst's voice. "Perkins! For the love of all that is holy, please tell me you haven't sent that image yet?"

"I'm sorry, sir." Perkins' voice was full of regret. "He was standing right behind me when the phone was switched on, so I had to do it. He wasn't very specific with what I could requisition on your behalf, though. I believe his exact words were, 'give Broadbent whatever he thinks will get the job done.' That gives us a fighting chance, at least."

Broadbent smiled. "It gives us more than a fighting chance, Perkins. Get me the Royal Armored Corps on the line."

United Kingdom, North Wales, Conwy Castle, Student Dormitory

Maxim was at the head of the pack as they charged up the stairs, laughing and shoving at each other as they raced to be the first back to the dorm. John had sent them up to unpack as soon as he saw Jean waiting in the lobby with her arms crossed.

"I wonder who's in trouble," Mischa chirped as they rounded the penultimate bend of the spiral.

"As long as it's not us, I don't care!" Craig quipped, shouldering his way past the twins to try to overtake Maxim.

The five teens ground to a halt when the familiar scent of Guardian James hit them. They finished their ascent at a walk, trying to act like they weren't surprised by his presence as they crossed the hallway.

"Morning, kids," James said, failing to hide his smile at their antics. "Did you all have a good time in the mountains?"

Halli and the twins suppressed their giggles. They'd had

a fun night making sure the British army guys didn't get a wink of sleep.

"It was an absolute *howl*, sir," Craig said in his terrible approximation of a British accent, bursting into a fit of laughter. It quickly spread to the whole group.

Guardian James looked at them like they'd lost their minds. "You'd better get yourselves into the dorm, kids. We've had a power outage and an attempted break-in today. You're all safer in there where we can keep an eye on you."

Their good mood evaporated in an instant.

"Was the intruder apprehended?" Maxim asked.

Guardian James shook his head. "That's why I'm here. You'll have either me or Guardian Donal outside the door at all times until we catch our would-be thief. Go on, your classmates are in there already."

They went into the dorm and found Tina, Ron, and Aleksi talking to Yana, Nestor and little Bai Hu on the flat-screen TV in the sleeping area.

The three turned from the TV to see who was coming when the door opened. When Maxim saw the worry etched across his friends' features, he crossed the room quickly and knelt by the bed they had sat on. "What happened here while we were gone?"

"I came up with a way to see what was on the phone. We were about to tell the others what we found."

"Maxim! Good to see you, my brother!" Nestor called from the screen.

"Hey, Maxim. Hey, everyone." Yana smiled. "Come and join the others so we can all know what they discovered."

"We will, Yana," Maxim told her. "But I want to know

how you three got around the problems you were so worried about."

The five Wechselbalg crammed themselves onto the bottom bunks nearest the TV and settled in to listen. Even Craig was solemn.

Tina looked around the group with wide eyes. "It wasn't anything special. I just noticed there was a Faraday room. It blocks signals. We were totally busted, but before that we saw the photo of Doctor Llewellyn's family being held hostage by men with guns."

"Do the adults know about the phone?" Maxim asked.

Tina, Ron, and Aleksi shook their heads.

Ron wrung his hands as he answered. "We need to make sure we're doing the right thing. What if we make things worse?"

"I don't see how it could be worse," Masha exclaimed. "Did you know there was a break-in attempt today?"

"No, but that explains a lot. We saw Doctor Llewellyn up here, or at least we saw someone we *think* was her," Aleksi said. "There's a secret passage behind the fireplace. Someone was up here just after the power cut."

"How do you know?" Craig asked.

"Because we were following her just before the power went out," Tina explained. "Jean sent us up here, and we saw the passage close."

"You must tell Ms. Dukes and your uncle," Yana stated firmly. "There are children in danger, and we cannot hope to help them by ourselves. Doctor Llewellyn may not be our enemy by choice, but that is perhaps worse." She wrapped a protective arm around Bai Hu and Nestor. "I am not a mother like Doctor Llewellyn, but I know that I would do *anything* to keep my family safe. Call us when it is over, please?"

"We will," Tina assured her friend.

Maxim nodded his agreement, as did everyone else in the dorm. "You are right, Yana. We will go to them now." He stood to leave. "I will call soon, Nestor. You can tell me about the fighter group then."

"Wait until I tell you of the game we devised!" Nestor exclaimed.

"I cannot wait to hear, brother," Maxim replied.

Nestor signed off, leaving the TV blank.

"I guess we'd better go face the music," Ron said weakly.

"It will be okay, my friend," Maxim said, patting Ron on the back. "The adults will know what to do." He hoped he sounded more confident than he felt.

"You did *what?*"

Tina had been nominated as spokesperson for the group, the rest of them thinking that the close relationship she had with both adults would deflect most of their ire.

They couldn't have been more wrong.

Jean's temper was a sight to behold. The students lined up in front of her, eyes down. John stood to the side, silent and disapproving.

"What *possessed* you to *sneak around* instead of coming to me or John when you first suspected Doctor Llewellyn?"

Tina told her pleadingly, "How could we accuse Doctor Llewellyn with no proof? What if we were wrong, and ruined her life?" She pulled her hand out of her pocket and handed the phone to Jean. "This is the real reason we were in the Faraday room…so we could look at this without alerting the bad guys. We weren't wrong. She *is* the saboteur, but she's being forced to do it. They've got her family."

Jean took the phone and switched it on. "There's proof on here?"

The students confirmed there was. The phone beeped in Jean's hand.

"A message." Jean's face hardened when she opened it. "Wait in your dorm. Do *not* leave it. I'm going to have a word with Doctor Llewellyn."

United Kingdom, North Wales, Conwy Castle, Laura Llewellyn's room

Laura sat in the chair by the bed with her head in her hands, exhausted. She couldn't keep this up much longer. The armor was complete, and her lies to MI5 about Jean's guns would soon come to light. *If only I knew who took the phone.*

Why hadn't Jean worked it out and confronted her, figured out that *she* was the one causing the breakdowns? The agent had been clear what would happen if she asked for help from TQB, but she had to try and get them involved somehow. It was her only hope of ever seeing her husband and children again.

But no, nothing. Her boss was too caught up in making sure the schedule for shutdown didn't go completely out of the window. She was afraid for Leo and Lexi; they were too young to understand any of the frightening things that were happening.

She wished she had never taken the job at TQB.

She was about to go to bed when the door slammed open and she looked up to meet the angry stare of Jean Dukes.

"You've got some explaining to do," Jean demanded roughly, throwing the missing phone onto the bed. "My students have just given me this." She pointed at the phone with a scowl. "Why didn't you tell me you were being coerced?"

"Because they're bloody *listening*, that's why!" Laura's heart fell. "They told me if I said anything then I wasn't going to see my family alive again." She couldn't hold back the tears any longer. The relief of not having to pretend everything was okay combined with the certainty that her family were lost to her forever wracked her and made her body shake. "You can just kill me now," she sobbed. "There's no need to wait for Bethany Anne to hear about it. I've got nothing left if I haven't got them."

Hurricane Jean calmed in a second. "Shit, I'm not going to let that happen, Laura. What kind of person do you think I am? BA is going to be pissed that you didn't ask for help, but she's not going to kill you." She sat heavily in the chair beside Laura's. "I just wish you'd come to me instead of pulling all the saboteur crap. I thought we were friends."

"That's exactly why I sabotaged things!" she cried. "I couldn't talk. I hoped you would find me out and then... I don't know what. After everything you and Bethany Anne have done for me? I didn't know *what* to do, okay?"

"We'll get them back," a gruff voice said. John stood in

the doorway, admiring the doorframe Jean had ruined as she came into the room. "Do you know who took them?" His voice was soft and calm, belying the deadliness Laura knew he was capable of.

"It's the government," she whispered, letting the tears fall. "MI5. They want your goddamn guns, and the Gauntlet armor with all its weapons."

Jean's nose wrinkled in distaste. "Why am I not surprised?" She turned to John in the doorway, holding out the phone. "There are two images on this. One old, and one new. Can you get with our IT guy on this? Find Laura's family and bring them back?"

John looked confused for a second. "IT...*oh*. Yeah, sure. What about you and the kids? I don't want to leave you here unprotected."

Jean laughed. "Do I look like a freaking *damsel*? Go and rescue Laura's family, hero-boy. We'll be fine until you get back."

He crossed the room in three strides and swept Jean into his arms. "How about a kiss for luck, seeing as you're sending me into battle?"

Laura did her best not to look and the moment was soon over.

John left for the courtyard and Jean sighed, her eyes firmly on John's behind. "I hate to see him leave, but I sure love to watch him go!"

"You're a lucky woman," Laura said, laughing through her tears.

Jean's eyebrow went up, only half-joking. "You're married and in shock, so I'll forgive you this once. That hunk of man is *all* mine, and I don't share."

Laura winked at Jean. "Gotcha. No ogling the eye-candy."

"I heard that!" John called back over his shoulder with a laugh. "I'm not a piece of meat, you know!"

"How else am I supposed to describe such prime beef-steak?" Jean said under her breath as he rounded the corner.

"I can *still* hear you!" John complained.

Laura snickered, the amusement turning to a yawn, which turned to tears again.

Jean steered her to the bed. "Get some sleep. We'll talk about everything MI5 made you do when you get up."

CHAPTER FIFTEEN

Q BBS *Meredith Reynolds*, All Guns Blazing

Diane nervously adjusted the skirt of her dress as she ascended the stairs to All Guns Blazing's viewing platform behind her sister. "Do you see them yet, DJ?"

Dorene unleashed a dazzling smile and waved to two young men seated at a table for four. "There they are, by the window. What do you think?"

They stood and waved back...one of them a little nervously, Diane thought.

Diane added her own smile of greeting, talking out of the side of her mouth to her sister as they crossed the floor. "I already told you that pilots are not my first choice when it comes to dating. If either of them is capable of talking about something other than themselves for more than a minute, I'll eat my hat. Narcissus had nothing on pilots, dear. *I* should know!"

Dorene hid a snigger, knowing full well what her twin thought about the fighter-pilot community. "Well at least we have dates! Let's enjoy dinner. We can talk about the students if Thomas and Leonard turn out to be a pair of bros."

Their dates scooched around the surrounding tables, and each pulled a chair out for the sisters.

"Good evening, ladies," the taller of the two men greeted them. He was blond and chiseled, where the other had dark hair and a kind face.

"Why, thank you, Thomas," Dorene said coyly, taking a seat. "How nice to be having dinner with a pair of gentlemen. You must be Leonard," she said to the other warmly, holding out a hand for him to shake. "Lovely to meet you. This is my sister, Diane."

Diane smiled and greeted the men, taking a close look at them both. Hers was the nervous one. He was a little shorter, a little less brash-looking than her sister's date, who she was absolutely certain would tick every box on her 'why pilots are a bad idea' list. She had the better deal, she thought. Hers looked a little more circumspect.

Diane decided to try and enjoy the evening. What was the worst that could happen? "Nice to meet you, Leonard," she said as he pushed the chair in for her. "That's one of my favorite names, you know! Like the character in *Star Journey*."

"I love *Star Journey*!" Leonard blushed, returning to his seat after helping Diane with hers.

"I think we all love *Star Journey*," she said approvingly.

"So, you two run a school?" Leonard asked Diane as Dorene and Thomas chatted beside them. "Tom's been telling me about having the trainees around."

"We do," she replied. It had been a long time since her

last date and Diane was feeling slightly nervous. "You're not one of the student mentors? I wondered why I didn't recognize you."

"No, not me." Leonard must have realized she was nervous because he smiled, touching her hand for a brief second before pulling his hand back. "It's okay, I'm not used to being set up on dates either. Thomas convinced me it would do me good to get out and meet someone. Can I get you a drink to start?" He jabbed a button on the table's console.

A server came over to them almost immediately. She gave them a thousand-watt smile, as if they were making her day by being there to enjoy themselves. "Hi! I'm Amy, and I'll be your waiter for the evening. What can I get for you all? Drinks?"

They gave Amy their drink orders.

"Can I get a menu?" Thomas asked.

Diane noted that he didn't say 'please'. *Strike one.*

Amy brought the drinks and a stack of menus for them to peruse. "Would you like me to activate the privacy filter?" she asked after they'd chosen their meals. "We've got a Guardian group booked in this evening, and they get pretty loud."

"Yes, that sounds like a good idea," Thomas said, returning to the anecdote he was telling Dorene without consulting any of them.

Strike two, buddy, Diane thought. She was glad he wasn't her date. There was only so much you could let slide for a pair of pretty eyes and a tight butt.

Not that Dorene seemed to mind. She listened to his sea story with rapt attention, head tilted to one side to get a better view of the pilot's deep blue eyes. The rest of the bar may as well have been empty, for all the attention Dorene paid it.

The chirpy waiter bounced off with their orders for steaks and fries, leaving the foursome to talk in privacy.

Diane turned her attention back to Leonard. "You're pretty quiet for a fighter jock, Leonard. What's your story?"

He buttered his roll as he replied, "I'm not a fighter jock, that's why. We can't all be brainless wonders. I mean, who wants to be stuffed in a tin can and fired *toward* the guns? Give me a nice safe transport gig any day."

Diane couldn't help but giggle at that. Maybe the evening wasn't going to be so bad after all.

The wait for dinner was short. Amy appeared quickly with the plates arranged on her arms in a feat of balance that impressed Diane. With the privacy filter only allowing the music through, the conversation turned to the food.

"I love how they get it just right here," Thomas remarked. "I've eaten steak all over the world, but nothing beats steak in space!"

"Sure," Diane agreed, cutting into her meat. "So, how do you two know each other?"

Thomas grinned. "That's a fun story."

"We grew up in the same neighborhood," Leonard said. "Didn't know each other, though."

"We enlisted on the same day, went to basic together. Stayed buddies even though we went our separate ways."

The two friends had a rhythm, like they'd told this story before. Thomas took a moment to top off the glasses again. Diane was surprised to see that they'd been there long enough to finish the bottle.

Amy appeared at the table with a tray of desserts, smiling as she passed them out. Diane looked over and saw Cheryl Lynn give a little wave from her booth. Diane gave her a surreptitious thumbs-up.

"Not that I have anything against kids being innovative, but the trainees are putting themselves at risk every time they climb into one of those experimental fighter Pods." Leonard had been talking to her, but she hadn't been paying attention. She pulled herself back to what he was saying, her good mood evaporating as the meaning of his words set in.

"Oh yes? Why is it so dangerous? I thought the Pods were perfectly safe."

Leonard broke into a laugh. He didn't see the warning in Diane's eyes. "The Pods are safe, it's the idiots flying them I worry about. Simulator training is all well and good, but there's no way kids should be taking them out for live-fire exercises."

Diane stood, placing her hands on the table in front of her so she could lean in. "*Live fire?* I sincerely hope that those trainees you're talking about aren't *my* students."

Leonard gulped, looking at Thomas for backup.

Thomas paled at the sight of the angry sisters. "Um... It's not as bad as he makes it sound. We just took them out to shoot up some asteroids."

Dorene leaned over and grabbed Thomas by the lapels. "Why, you no-good low-down... You let the students do *what*? Are you cerebrally challenged?"

Diane threw her napkin down in disgust. "*Strike three*, you're out. This date is *over*."

. . .

United Kingdom, North Wales, Temporary HQ Opposite Conwy Castle

Broadbent peered anxiously at the map on the table, poking at the little die-cast models surrounding the castle one of the men had made from children's building blocks while he waited impatiently for Perkins to speak.

A sudden squawk from the speaker startled him, then it emitted Perkins' voice. "Ground forces are in position, sir."

He gave his head a shake before thumbing the button to answer. "Roger, Perkins. Advise on Challenger positions, over."

"Challengers are expected in T minus two hours, sir. Bloody expressway, *again*."

Broadbent waited for Perkins to release the button.

"Sorry, sir. I can't get my head around this silly walkie-talkie idea. Oh…dammit. Over."

"Our digital comms are compromised, Perkins. The radios are necessary." Broadbent sighed. "If the expressway doesn't clear up within the next fifteen minutes, radio and tell them to dump the transport and come overland. I'm about to move into position. I'll be dark until it's over, one way or another. Over." He released the button, then pressed it down again quickly before he could change his mind. "Perkins."

"Yes, sir?"

He paused. "If I don't make it out of this slapdash folly, it's been good knowing you, old chap."

This time Perkins was the one struggling to speak. "Be careful, won't you, sir?"

Broadbent dropped the walkie-talkie on the table and left the tent. He found the team he'd asked for waiting, fully loaded for an assault. They were dressed in black, faces painted and bristling with weapons.

They joked and jostled one another; the bravado of men about to go into battle.

Most of them would die tonight.

United Kingdom, North Wales, Student Dormitory, Conwy Castle

"Someone's coming," Halli whispered, diving under the covers.

"Lights out was fifteen minutes ago. Who would be coming in here?" Aleksi replied, not having the Wechselbalg gift of enhanced senses.

"It is Ms. Dukes?" Maxim asked sleepily.

Jean opened the door, letting in a sliver of warm yellow light from the hall. She was no longer angry, but clearly still bothered by something.

"Kids, are you still awake?"

Tina sat up and switched the light on. "Where's John? Has something else happened?"

Jean shook her head. "No, he's gone to get Doctor Llewellyn's family. He'll be back soon. He's just having fun teaching the Brits why kidnapping and extortion is a bad idea. I wanted to check in on you all, since it's been a hell of a day. How are you all holding up?"

A mumble of noncommittal replies washed around the students.

Jean nodded. "We'll make sure there's someone for you to talk to when we get home. I wanted to come and tear another strip off your hides, but I realized that you did a good thing—even if the way you all went about it wasn't very well thought out."

Tina was about to argue when she saw Jean go distant, her eyes unfocused like she was somewhere else. "Who was that?" she asked when Jean came back to herself.

"I've got to go. You kids get back in bed now. I'll come and see you when I've dealt with this problem."

"Jean, what is it?" Tina was alarmed now.

Jean did a double-take, studying Tina closely. "You've never called me by my first name before."

"And I won't again if you don't tell us what's going on!" She drew herself up to her full height, wishing she had a pair of her mom's heels so she could look Jean straight in the eye.

Jean shook her head with a wry smile. "Not this time, Tina. I haven't got time for explanations right now. There's a situation outside the castle walls I have to deal with. You kids are the best, but you're still kids and the safest place for you is here in the dorm. You'll all stay here, and this time *don't* disobey me. Am I making myself clear?"

Tina stamped her foot and went back to her bunk sulkily. "Fine, but we could *help*. We're not untrained children, you know."

Jean was already leaving. "I know, but I've got this. You get some rest, you hear me?"

The door closed behind her, leaving them in darkness, and they heard a click as she locked it from the outside. Tina waited a few minutes, then crept out of her bunk and went to kneel at the door. Maxim followed, and they pressed their ears up against it to hear what Jean was saying to Guardian James.

"To the west and the south, in an arc." The solid oak door muffled Jean's voice, but Tina could just make out what she was saying. "No heavy ordnance, just manpower."

Guardian James spoke so softly she couldn't make his reply. She waited for Jean to speak again.

"I could use you and Guardian Donal in the Black Eagles. I can hold the front until John gets back. Give it twenty minutes. Let the kids fall asleep, then come and find me."

The twenty minutes crawled by agonizingly slowly. Craig was a pressure cooker, primed to explode by the time they heard Guardian James walk away.

"I thought he would never go!" he gasped when they heard the elevator doors close behind the Guardian. He crouched between Tina and Maxim. "So...our illustrious leaders. What's the plan?"

"The first thing we need to do is get this door open. Masha, can you pick this lock?"

"It's more complicated than the one on Doctor Llewellyn's desk drawers. It might take a while."

"We haven't got time for that," Maxim said softly. "The enemy is at our door, and everyone except Ms. Dukes and the Guardians will die if we don't get out of here. We need to help them. We will break it down. Get out of the way."

Tina cringed as he took a run-up, leaping just before he crashed into the iron-banded oak to maximize his momentum. His shoulder hit the door with a dull *thud* and he bounced back, knocking Halli over.

"*Gott Verdammt!*" he exclaimed, having heard John say it more than a few times over the last week. "Sorry, Halli."

"I'm okay," the girl said, springing up. "Hey, you damaged the door. I'm impressed!"

"Yeah, you did okay, Maxim. The band on the middle has cracked, and the hinges are bent." Tina was examining the door. "Come and put those nanocytes to work. I think you can pull it off the frame with a few good tugs."

She stepped away from the door, taking Ron and Aleksi with her.

Maxim, Halli and Craig all grabbed on where they could and looked around for the twins.

"You don't seriously think I'm going to break my nails on that, do you?" Mischa proclaimed.

"No, you two just sit there. Don't worry your pretty little heads," Craig snarked. He kept muttering, knowing full well they could hear him, "It's not like you have super-strength or anything."

Masha joined him on the loose board. "I at least will help," she said, nudging his shoulder with hers.

Back and forth they worked the loose boards, prying the nails that held them together free an inch at a time. It took a few minutes, but soon they had enough boards removed to compromise the integrity of the door.

"I hope this door was a replacement and not a genuine antique," Tina said as she stacked the boards the Wechsel-balg kids passed back to them.

Ron made a soft noise in the back of his throat.

Tina winced. "It's original? Well, hopefully it can be put back together afterwards. We only broke one board."

There was a clang as the cracked iron band fell to the floor with nothing to hold it up. Their way clear, the kids went through the hole in the door, their attempt at stealth more comical than effective given the noise they made falling into the hallway.

"Ow, watch it!" Tina squealed as someone trod on her hand. She got up quickly and dusted herself off.

"Where is the secret passage?" Ron asked, scanning the walls. "Never mind, now that I know it's there it'll be easy to find. Fireplace, yeah?" He went over and started the same prodding and pressing process Aleksi had performed earlier.

"It's not a pressure pad, Ron," Aleksi said. "I couldn't work out how to open it at all."

Ron grinned and pulled hard on the wall sconce beside the fireplace. "Ta-*daaa*!" A shower of dust fell from the sconce and landed on his head, but nothing else happened. "Aw, man! It must be something else. Try everything!"

They all went around the hallway pulling on the wall sconces between.

There was a *crunch* and Craig blurted, "Whoops."

They all turned to see him with a wall sconce in his hand. It was no longer attached to the wall.

"*Craig!*" Tina was appalled. "How did that happen?"

Craig shrugged. "I thought twisting them might work. I dunno, it just came off in my hand."

Masha snickered. "Only you would do such a thing, Craig."

"What is this?" Maxim asked, moving in for a closer look at the crests carved into the mantle pillars behind Craig. "They are not the same on both sides. Look!"

They crowded around Maxim. The roaring lions on the crests were almost identical, but one was set at a slightly different angle.

Aleksi hit his forehead with the heel of his hand. "How could I have missed this?"

Ron scratched his head. "Where are they looking? That's where we'll find the release mechanism."

Eight pairs of eyes followed the path from the lions' eyes to the tapestry on the opposite wall. Craig was the first one there, grabbing the bottom edge of the tapestry. "It's not attached like the others. The corner is loose."

"I'll go," Ron volunteered. "You've had all the fun without me so far."

"How do you know the others are attached?" Mischa enquired, tilting her head with curiosity.

Craig grinned. "The other day, I was going to hide behind one and jump out on whoever walked past first," he confessed. He lifted the heavy tapestry, allowing Ron to duck under and examine the wall behind.

"Eureka!" Ron blurted a few seconds later. There was a grinding sound as the fireplace swung open. "Where does this thing lead, anyway?"

Tina was the first to enter the dark tunnel. "I don't know, but it won't be to wherever the adults are. Come on, let's go." She pulled her tablet out and activated the torch function before taking the first step down the narrow twisting staircase its light revealed.

The others followed, turning on their own torch apps. The passage wound on and on, sometimes level, sometimes stairs, but always descending. There was a short landing between each flight of stairs, and they noted the levels of the facility as they went. They passed locked doors, and the occasional bench carved into the wall. There were boxes on the walls above the benches.

"They're peepholes," Ron remarked when they passed the second one and his torch caught it. "Should we look?"

"No!" Halli scoffed. "What if it goes into a bathroom or something? Gross!"

Maxim didn't find any of it funny. "Come on, we need to find an exit. We've got to be getting close to the bottom of the castle by now."

They came to a halt as the stairs ended suddenly, culminating in a dark, dank room carved out of the rock. There was no exit and no windows, just five crates of varying large sizes lined up against the back wall. The light from the tablets sent shadows skittering across their faces, revealing everyone's wide eyes and drawn expressions.

Maxim was the first to say it. "We are not in the castle anymore."

"No crap." Tina laughed. She shone her light onto the crates. "*Holy...*" She stopped in her tracks. "You have to see this!"

"What is it?" Ron asked, taking a closer look. "Oh, *please* don't let me be dreaming! Is that..." He slapped himself across the face, the sudden sharp noise startling the others.

"What did you do that for?" Mischa fumed. "You scared the life out of us!"

Ron blinked to clear his head. "I had to make sure I was awake. *Look at the stamp!* They're Project Gauntlet prototypes. They shouldn't even *be* here!"

"What is Project Gauntlet?" Masha asked, reading the small stamp on the side of the nearest crate.

"Yeah, and why does Fanboy here look like all his Christmases have come at once?" Craig snickered, waving a hand in front of Ron's face.

Aleksi knelt by the crates, placing a reverent hand on the side of the largest one. "Get one of these crates open and you'll see," he said in an awed voice. "I'm with Ron... this is an amazing discovery."

Craig did as he was bid, ripping the lid off the smallest crate like he was pulling off the top of a yogurt carton. He began dancing wildly in his excitement, throwing shadows everywhere. "Oh. My. God. Look at this!"

He dropped the lid so they could all see the gleaming suit of armor within. They all gasped at the array of weaponry attached to the solid carapace.

"That is some heavy ordnance," Maxim said with a low whistle. "I see lasers, mini-missiles... Oh, wow, are those Jean Dukes guns?"

Ron moved closer to examine them. "No, just standard projectile guns."

"Those are big guns," Masha said in an awestruck voice. "Hey, do you think we'll get these when we graduate and go into the Guardians?"

"I've never seen *anything* as cool as this armor," Craig breathed. "I want to try one on!"

"*NO!*" everyone shouted at once.

"We need to tell Jean," Tina insisted. "They could use this armor right now. It could be a gamechanger."

The others agreed, and she called Jean on her tablet.

Jean was not impressed when she saw the cave in the background of the video call. "Why are you kids out of the dorm? I told you to stay put. I was *very* clear!"

Tina spoke quickly before Jean lost her temper completely. "We're not defenseless kids, Jean! We heard you talking to Guardian James. We couldn't just *sit* there

162

while we're about to be attacked, not after Mongolia. You have to understand!"

Jean was silent for a long moment.

When she spoke, it was a different Jean Dukes who addressed them. "Fine. You want to be treated like adults, you get to *work* like adults. We need to build a defense to repel these assholes. Get yourselves up to the Pod and start stripping the guns." Gone was the teacher, and in her place was the fearsome warrior ready to do battle to protect her own.

Tina smirked. "We won't need to strip the Pod. We found something you're going to be happy to see." She spun her tablet around so Jean could see the open crate.

Jean was flabbergasted. "*What the...* How did you get that armor? I haven't even *built* it yet! Where are you, Tina? Please tell me you're still inside the castle."

She turned the tablet back around so Jean could see her again. "Kind of. There's a secret passage leading down from the tower. It goes from the fireplace in the hall, all the way down under the castle. We're in a cave at the bottom."

Tina saw the glint in Jean's eye as she spoke. "Get those crates unpacked. I'll be there soon."

United Kingdom, North Wales, Llandudno, Passenger Pod Over the Great Orme

John looked down at the mine entrance as he fastened his armor. "Are you sure this is the right place? It doesn't look like an MI5 black site. Look at all the civilians."

"I am certain that this is the location to which the Llewellyn family were taken," the Pod's EI replied. "This is the Great Orme, and beneath it is a Bronze Age copper mine which is open to tourists—like every other location of mild interest in Wales. Scans indicate an area that is not shown on the available maps."

"That'll be where the stupid eel-eating shart detectors are keeping Laura's family," he growled.

"The evidence certainly points that way," the EI concurred. "I am picking up three distinct heat signatures in one of the rear caves, surrounded by approximately a hundred more in the surrounding area."

John gripped the console. "*Spineless cowards.* One hundred guards for one man and two small children?" When he heard a crunch he looked down; the front panel of the console had crumpled in his hands like a piece of paper.

"Your blood pressure is rising. Perhaps instead of damaging the Pod you would prefer to take your anger out on the guards below? Just a suggestion."

John laughed, letting go of the crushed metal. "A suggestion, *HA*! What is it with you EIs? You're all *way* too quirky to be programs." He zoomed in on the viewscreen, seeing a few families clustered around their cars in the floodlit parking lot. "It looks like it's been busy down there today. *Gott Verdammt*, that means I'll have to be careful. Can you do something to get the staff out of there?"

"Already done. I have sent a bomb threat to the local police station, and they are contacting the tour operators to tell them to evacuate as we speak."

"Ok, good. Gives me time to prepare." He went over to the weapons locker and stood there musing over what to take with him. "Huh. This isn't as fun without the guys around." He looked regretfully at the drawer with the grenades nestled in protective foam. "Not today."

"It is well documented that humorous exchanges between operatives before engagement lowers blood pressure and anxiety levels," the EI put in. "Perhaps I could tell you a joke? I am programmed to provide levity in a tense situation."

"I'll bite. Go ahead," John replied skeptically, shrugging a back harness on. "Might not be able to shoot," he muttered to himself, strapping on the holsters for his Jean Dukes Specials.

"What has four legs and one arm?"

He pulled on the harness to make sure the straps were in place and slid a matched pair of short swords into its sheaths. "I don't know, what has four legs and one arm?"

"A happy attack dog."

"Woof, woof." John chortled. "Not the manly banter I'm used to, but not a bad effort for a computer program."

"I am slightly offended by that."

"*That* is exactly what I was talking about." He ran his fingers over the smooth grain of the wood on his pistols' handgrips reverently before placing them in the holsters. "Maybe I'll get an arm or two along the way, maybe I won't. But I'll tell you this: if those children have been harmed in any way, I won't stop until I have the heads of everyone responsible."

"A reasonable reaction, sir," the EI replied.

He scowled. "I'm not happy with how long the tourists are taking to leave. Is there another entrance I can use?"

A pause, then the EI spoke. "There is a small tunnel on the cliff which leads to the rear of the cave system, away from the public areas, but it will be a tight squeeze. Many of the tunnels in the cave system are too small for anybody bigger than a child."

John went over to the console. "Show me." He scrutinized the image of the narrow aperture in the rock. "There's no way I'm getting through that tiny crack. Looks like the front way is the only option." He made a face, opening the grenade drawer again and taking two. "Better to have them and not need them than need them and not have any." He added a couple of teargas canisters and a smoke-bomb to be on the safe side. "Call Jean so I can let her know I've found the Llewellyns."

Jean's face appeared on the screen. "Hey, have you found Laura's family?"

John breathed deeply at the sound of her voice. "Yeah, they're being held in an old copper mine up the coast from the castle."

Jean grinned. She had a familiar light in her eyes, one that usually meant Saint Payback was about to visit someone in need of a lesson. "Go get them, then! What are you waiting for? If you don't get back here soon you'll miss the party."

"Party?" He saw the kids in the background, pulling what looked like a set of Pricolici-sized armor to pieces. "What's going on? Are you and the kids in danger?"

Jean shook her head to reassure him. "MI5 has brought in the army, but we'll be fine until you get back." She moved the camera to show him the action in the room. The kids were deeply absorbed in building something dangerous-looking from pieces of the armor and a big lens. "They're safe, and getting some practical experience to boot. I'll talk to Bethany Anne and get her to okay the plan. Hey, check this out!"

The camera wobbled while she passed it to Halli. When it steadied, he saw his love in the most badass armor he'd ever seen outside Bethany Anne's collection. When she pressed something, the guns on her shoulders did a little dance and the lights of the targeting lasers bounced around as she posed. "What do you think?"

John let out a low whistle. "Whoa, are those... Is that the Gauntlet armor? I didn't think it had reached this stage yet."

Jean winked. "It hadn't, but MI5 shot themselves in the ass when they forced Laura to make it for them. She was hiding it underneath the castle." An alarm went off in the background. "Got to go. They're starting the approach, and we still need to get this laser cannon mounted."

"If you're sure," John told her, pulling a jacket on to hide his weapons. The armor was very distracting.

Jean waved at him. "I can read your mind, John Grimes! Go rescue those poor people. I can manage here." She blew him a kiss and the screen went blank.

He took the Pod down, landing behind a rocky outcropping for cover. As he left the Pod, he gave his instructions to the EI via the earpiece he'd picked up on his way out. "As soon as I leave, take the Pod back up. Don't let anyone see it. Stay in contact, and be ready when I call. The Llewellyns might be injured."

"Of course," the EI replied. "You should hurry. The police are on their way to deal with our imaginary bomb."

"I don't think you thought that one through properly." He walked toward the mine entrance, avoiding eye contact with the remaining tourists in the parking lot. One man looked like he was going to approach, but John changed his mind with a little *push* of fear.

It had the intended effect; the last few people were quick to leave. He stalked to the empty lobby where a nervous young woman was pulling a metal concertina gate closed across the entrance to the mine.

She looked up at him as he reached the gate. "Tours are over for the day, sir," she said in a lilting accent. "You'll have to come back tomorrow, you will."

"The police are approaching the mine," the EI said in his ear.

"I'm not here for a tour," he said gruffly, taking the gate out of her hand. "I'm here about the bomb."

The young woman was shaking. Her eyes bulged with fear both at the mention of a bomb and his proximity to her. John could hear her heart racing.

"Don't worry," he looked at her name badge, "Kaylie. I'm here to take care of it," he said. Her relief was palpable. He gently but firmly deposited her on the outside of the gate and pulled it shut behind himself. "Keys?"

She handed them over wordlessly.

He smiled as he locked the gate. "Good girl. Now you get out of here, do you hear me?"

He turned and started down the tunnel at a jog. "You'd better be able to keep me from getting lost in here," he said to the EI as he came to a signpost at an intersection in the tunnels.

"Follow the arrows. There is a tunnel off the main tour route which leads to the target location."

It wasn't long before he found the main cave and the

door marked 'Personnel Only'. The tunnel beyond was dark, but that didn't bother him. He didn't need light to see by, but the enemy would not know that.

He came to another door, not needing the EI to guide him anymore. He could sense the men waiting behind it.

"How close are the Llewellyns?" he asked the EI. "Is it safe to use a grenade down here?"

"The tone of your voice suggests you already know the answer to that."

He sighed theatrically, selecting a less lethal alternative instead. "You're taking all the fun out of this."

"Go ahead and use the grenades if you like. I'm sure you can survive a mountain falling on your head. I'm not sure what the Queen will make of it, though."

"Just you wait until we get back, Snarky McSnarkerson. I'm going to have ADAM make it so you can only speak French."

The EI had no comeback.

Satisfied with the silence, John lifted his heavy boot and slammed the door off its hinges, *pushing* fear ahead of him in a thick wave.

It's going to suck to be them in about thirty seconds, John thought, one side of his mouth lifting mischievously as he threw the activated teargas and smoke-bombs into the room.

The enemy was woefully underprepared for dealing with a Queen's Bitch, and even less prepared for the right-eous anger of John Grimes.

He marched in with his JD Specials drawn and fingers already stroking the triggers, and took out the coughing and spluttering soldiers before they knew what had hit them.

"Where are the Llewellyns?" he asked the EI as the sound of the enemy dying faded.

"Two rooms ahead," the EI replied.

"How many of these asshats are left?"

"You have cleaned this room up nicely. I estimate there are another sixty between you and the Llewellyns."

"Rinse and repeat until desired results are attained," he quipped. The EI was conspicuously silent. "Nope, definitely not the same without the guys to laugh at my one-liners," he muttered.

He was saved the bother of kicking the next door in when it opened outwards and spilled a bunch of pale-faced soldiers out into the room. They huddled together with their rifles at the ready, backlit by the soft yellow glow from the door behind them.

"You all look appropriately scared," he told them. "If you leave now, I'll say nothing more."

"Screw you!" one of them shouted, firing wildly into the darkness.

John grinned, raising his guns and *pushing* the fear ahead of him again. "I think you meant to say, 'screw you, *sir,*'" he told them, stepping forward.

CHAPTER SIXTEEN

United Kingdom, North Wales, Inside Conwy Castle

"This bit here," Tina demanded. "No, it *has* to be aligned correctly!" She huffed with frustration as the rig slipped again. "Where is Maxim?"

She turned to find him on the other side of the lab by Guardian James, watching Halli assist the older Wechselbalg into one of the armor suits. "Maxim! Get over here and help!"

Maxim reluctantly dragged himself over to where Tina, Ron and Aleksi were working. "Tell me again why we are doing this to perfectly good armor?" he asked skeptically.

Tina's mouth pursed. "Because we don't need Pricolici armor, unless there's something you're not telling us? Now hold this *Gott Verdammt* lens in place while I align the lasers!"

Maxim did as he was told, mumbling under his breath, "You're mean when you're working."

"Complain all you like, Maxim," she chided. "Just hold the freaking lens!"

Jean came by, all fastened into the smaller suit of armor. "How's it going?"

Ron looked up from where he was micro-soldering the bunch of wires he'd pulled out of the laser guns to a circuit board. "All good, Ms. Dukes. Aleksi has almost finished programming the settings for the laser canon and the projectile guns, and missile launchers are already fixed to the battlements."

"We just need to get this rig secure, or the cannon will blow *us* up instead of the enemy." Tina wrinkled her nose.

Jean's face softened. "You kids don't have to go out there. I'll understand if you want to leave with Doctor Llewellyn and the rest of the evacuees."

Maxim frowned and protested, "I will not stand by while evil remains."

"Lift that lens!" Tina screeched.

"Sorry," he said, bracing his arms again. "Ms. Dukes?" he asked tentatively. "What does it feel like, to know you have taken a life?"

"That's a very personal question, Maxim." She took a deep breath. "Stop what you're doing for a minute, all of you, and gather round."

"But…" Tina spluttered. "The lens!"

"This is important, Tina," Jean stated. "We are up against an army of hundreds here. Make no mistake—the enemy does not care if you are children."

"Sorry," Tina apologized. "I'm listening."

Jean leaned back against the workbench opposite the one they were using. "We could abandon the facility, but that's not how we roll. There are innocent people here who will die today if we don't step up and defend this place." She pointed to the scientists and techs rushing through last minute preparations for the evacuation. "*These* people. You're all growing up—too fast if you ask me—but this is the situation the Brit bastards have put us in."

She looked them in the eyes, one after another. "If you can't handle it, that's fine. Not everyone is meant to be on the sharp edge of things. But I'll tell you something: I will fight to protect every single person in this castle. I fight to protect our Queen, to stop our fledgling empire being attacked by the greedy fat cats down here. I would fight and I would *die* for each and every one of you kids."

"Same!" Guardian James called as he fastened the last piece of his armor.

Aleksi held a hand up for permission to speak. "What about the soldiers? They are just following orders."

Jean sniffed at that. "I'm sure you've all heard at least one person back home say this, but I'm going to make sure you all understand. *All it takes for evil to succeed is for good people to stand by and do nothing.* 'I was only following orders' is not an excuse for committing atrocities. They know there are kids here, and yet they're moving into position to attack us as we speak. All so they can get their slimy hands on our technology."

Tina snorted. "Not on my watch!"

"Nor mine!" Maxim cried fervently.

Ron and Aleksi agreed.

"Good," Jean said. "I'm glad we all know where we stand. Now, can I give you a hand with that cannon or have you got it?" Her tablet bleeped. "Oh, hang fire a minute. John's calling me."

United Kingdom, North Wales, Llandudno, The Great Orme

John approached the last door, the one he hoped the Llewellyn family were behind. He grasped the heavy padlock and pulled it free with no effort whatsoever, then opened the door.

Hugh Llewellyn pushed the two small children behind him, protecting them with his body. "You leave us be!"

John held up a hand, keeping his voice low so he didn't scare the kids any more than they already were. "It's okay, Hugh. My name is John Grimes. Laura sent me. I'm not with the bad guys."

Hugh narrowed his eyes, John's American accent not what he was expecting. "What're you doing in here, then, eh?"

"Getting you and the kids the hell out, Hugh," John replied calmly. He knelt to make himself less threatening and spoke directly to the children. "You must be Leo and Lexi. Your mom sent me to rescue you and your dad. I'm going to take you to her, okay?"

The EI spoke into his ear. "The police have arrived, and are cordoning off the parking lot outside."

"Is there something nearby you can blow up safely to cause a distraction?"

"I can do that."

"Good. Do it, then bring the Pod to the entrance as soon as they leave."

The children clung mutely to their father's legs, dazed with shock from the trauma of their ordeal. John got to his feet and gestured to Hugh. "Follow me. You should probably cover their eyes," he added to Hugh in a low voice. "It's pretty messy out there." He turned back to the door, making sure it was safe to proceed.

Hugh picked up the children, one in each arm, and followed him, pressing their heads into his neck so they didn't see the gore-washed rooms beyond. "Jesus, what happened in here? I heard the racket, but..."

John said nothing, letting Hugh draw his own conclusions. He felt a brief ripple in the ground as the EI created the distraction and started walking toward the exit. "Come on, we haven't got long before things start getting difficult."

United Kingdom, North Wales, Conwy Castle, Battlements, East Barbican

Mischa growled in frustration. "Ow! That's *another* nail gone!" She threw the wrench down in frustration, stamping her foot. "If I wanted to be a spanner chimp I would have made more of an effort in engineering class!"

Craig cackled. "I think you mean a grease monkey, Mischa. Let me see. I'm done here." He put his welding torch down, then leaned over and applied his own wrench to the problem bolt. "There, it's tight."

"I'm done with the hairy-ass projectile guns over here," Masha called from farther along the parapet. "Mischa, quit whining about your nails! This is *war*, not a catwalk, and if we don't get this done right now we won't be ready when they bring the cannon up."

"I can't believe we get to fire a laser cannon," Craig marveled.

Mischa stuck out her tongue at him. "Nobody will be firing it. Ron and Aleksi will control it from their tablets. If you're lucky, you might get to fire the projectile guns. Just keep your hands away from the boom-y end, hey?"

Craig stuck his tongue out in return. "My hands grew back quicker than your nails are going to. Especially if you don't improve your 'spanner chimp' efforts." Mischa punched him in the arm. "OW!"

"Serves you right," Mischa said, rubbing her knuckles.

"*Both* of you, quit it," Masha hissed. "Look!" She pointed across the river to where six tanks were pulling up on a grassy expanse between the river and the road. "Where are Ms. Dukes and the others? It's starting."

"I'll call," Craig said, dropping his wrench and fishing in his pocket for his tablet.

"No need, I'm here," Jean said from behind them, and all three of them jumped out of their skins. She placed the box of equipment she was carrying on the floor next to them. "Is the cradle ready?"

"Yes, ma'am," they replied smartly.

Maxim, Halli, Tina, and Ron arrived on the parapet, carefully carrying the laser rig they'd built.

"Watch that lens!" Jean warned. "We haven't got a spare. Get this set up. I'll be back to check on you as soon as I've programmed Bethany Anne's Pod to take out those tanks if they fire on us." She sped off, not waiting for a reply from them.

Tina clapped her hands the way her mother did when she wanted to get people moving. "You heard Jean, let's *go!* Lift the rig into the cradle. We've got a laser cannon to bring online!"

They lifted the bulky apparatus onto the heavily reinforced bars.

"Next, attach here, here, and here," she commanded, pointing at various spots where the rig and the cradle met. Craig stepped forward with the welding torch in one hand and the wrench in the other. "Pick *one*, Craig," she told him.

She whirled around. "Aleksi and Ron, are you up and running yet?"

Aleksi nodded. "The laser cannon and the mini-missiles are linked to the Bootstrapping app. I have the EI feeding it real-time data using TQB satellites so we will know the enemy's precise movements at all times. All we have to do is launch the end phase of the game when they start to move in."

Tina smiled. "Good. Now we wait on word from Jean to begin."

CHAPTER SEVENTEEN

U nited Kingdom, North Wales, Conwy Castle Courtyard, Bethany Anne's Pod

Bethany Anne's eyes popped out at Jean's report. "Those low-down snaky little spam-humpers! Jesus, Jean, that's a *lot* of troops approaching your location. Do you need me to come down there? I'm a little preoccupied with Majestic, but I'll drop everything if you and the kids are in danger."

Jean shook her head. "Go stamp those Illuminati wannabes out, BA. We're good. The armor Laura had stashed will be enough to get us through. Hang on... Look at this!" She sent the video she'd made while the kids were building the laser cannon.

Bethany Anne gave a low whistle. "Wow, that's one kick-ass cannon."

"I know, right? They've come up with other stuff, too. We've got this, and the kids will be fine. If it gets to the point where I think they're in danger, we'll evacuate them up to the *Meredith Reynolds* immediately. Until then, I'd like them to get a chance to feel empowered. I've heard them chatting about what happened in Mongolia. It knocked their confidence in their own abilities a little."

Bethany Anne nodded. "You're right, but don't tell Diane and Dorene I said that. You know they're going to give us all an ass-chewing for this, don't you?"

Jean laughed. "I'd like to see them try. There's always an airlock nearby if they get too sassy." Bethany Anne laughed at that, and Jean continued, "What would help is if you make it clear to the army that they are about to attack our children. At least give them a chance to turn back. I don't want to kill military people who aren't aware of what their brass have gotten them into."

"Sure." Bethany Anne looked away a minute. When she returned her eyes were red. "Jean? ADAM has just told me that all approaching units have been instructed to take you out and subdue the kids by 'whatever means necessary.' They want the armor, and they want your guns. They don't care."

Jean's face set in a hard mask. "Extreme prejudice it is, then," she growled.

"Fine by me. Have fun!" Bethany Anne's face vanished from the screen.

Jean stepped out of Bethany Anne's Pod and into the courtyard where Guardians James and Donal waited. She took a second to watch as the Pod rose into the sky and the exterior rippled and faded out of sight as the prototype cloaking device activated.

Jean grinned. "You know, BMW might not be able to find their own asses with two hands and a radar, but they manage to come up with some stuff that amazes the hell out of me!"

The two Wechselbalg laughed heartily.

"Come on, we'd better check on the kids."

As they were about to go inside, Donal stopped dead and sniffed the air. "Get *DOWN!*"

Jean heard the whistle of an incoming missile in the next second and dived. "*Gott Verdammt!*" Her quick reactions saved her from a burning metal shower; the Pod pucked the missile just before it began its downward arc.

"They're moving in!" Donal cried. "East barbican gates!"

She tucked and rolled to her feet, pistols drawn. "Oh *hell*, no! *THAT DOES IT*," she roared, dialing her pistols up to eight. "*I'm going to make them all wish they'd never been born!*"

United Kingdom, North Wales, Temporary HQ Opposite Conwy Castle

Broadbent held the field glasses up to his eyes, watching as the first missile was intercepted. When the burning debris fell on the castle, he held a hand to his stomach to quell his physical reaction to what was happening.

He clearly saw the children on the parapet at the east barbican, although for the life of him he couldn't figure out why TQB would allow them to be there while the castle was being attacked. But he had orders, and he would carry them out to the letter. Let nobody say that he didn't have the stomach to do his duty.

The first wave of soldiers moved into position at the

base of the wall, ready to blow the gate and storm the castle as soon as the missile hit the east barbican wall.

Broadbent watched in disbelief as a projectile came out of the sky and detonated the next missile in midair. His nightmare got worse barely a minute later when the barbican gates slammed open and his troops began to die in misty explosions. It was the engineering woman, Jean Dukes! She was shooting those blasted guns of hers, and the audio channel was filled with screams and gurgles.

He pressed the button on his walkie-talkie with a shaky thumb. "Perkins? What the hell is going on? Over."

"It's not going well so far, is it, sir?" the analyst replied. "Over."

"You have a gift for understatement, Perkins. Perhaps a job in politics would suit you after the MOD give us both our marching orders. Over."

Perkins harrumphed. "Nobody warned us about the Dukes woman, sir. Over."

"Send in the reinforcements. That ought to do the job, Perkins. Let's get this over and done with before someone from *up there* comes *down here*. It's only a matter of time, and we're not going to be getting those guns from her. We need to get what we can and scarper."

"The armor at least, sir," Perkins agreed.

Broadbent trained his field glasses on the bridge where the Special Forces teams were getting into position, but he couldn't see a thing. "*Damn* those boys are good," he muttered. He swung back to the castle, his heart falling when he saw the short work the Dukes woman was making of his men.

Broadbent didn't think it could get any worse, but then

a hail of projectiles hammered down from the battlements where he'd seen the children. Nothing happened, then the Dukes woman turned to the bridge and fired her infernal pistols.

He heard a low *BOOM* come from the direction of the river.

The rail bridge collapsed in front of his eyes, crushing the Special Forces teams as over a thousand tons of concrete and cast iron crashed into the river.

His shock turned to rage when he saw both the children and the Dukes woman celebrating.

Broadbent worked his mouth as he processed what he was seeing. "*Those little bastards!* They're *dancing!* Perkins, send every single asset we have in. *TELL THOSE POXY ARTILLERY MUPPETS TO GET OFF THEIR LAZY BEHINDS AND DO SOMETHING WITH THOSE BLOODY TANKS!*"

"You're shouting, sir," Perkins complained.

He took a breath to calm himself. "My apologies, Perkins. I asked for mercy for those little monsters, and just look what they've done! Time for a change of plan. Patch me in to Myerscough. Over and out."

The walkie-talkie crackled. "Myerscough here. What is going on down there? Looks like a godforsaken shambles! Over."

"This whole damned operation has been a shambles," Broadbent muttered to himself. He thumbed the button again. "Get me three of your best men and an airlift, Captain. I'm going in as soon as I can get a ride. Over."

CHAPTER EIGHTEEN

B attlements, East Barbican, Conwy Castle
The puck slammed into the missile high above the courtyard, creating a brief shower of molten metal that lit the twilight like a firework.

"Comms active, stations *ready!*" Maxim commanded, taking the lead. He glanced at the group, seeing grim determination painted on their faces. He knew his own would look the same if he could see it.

Craig and Mischa took the projectile guns, and Masha and Halli took the improvised missile launchers. Tina tended to last minute checks on the cannon, making sure each of the eight lasers sat flush with the lens, and that there were no scratches in the ceramic polymer Ron had cooked up to coat the sides of the flat-topped cone to prevent the concentrated laser beam from splitting and burning them all.

"I don't know how we managed to convince Jean to let us build this incredibly dangerous piece of equipment," Craig remarked offhand.

"You don't know?" Mischa called. "We just had to promise not to let *you* go near it!"

"Hey," Craig protested as they all dissolved into laughter. "I can handle a laser!"

"Come on, Craig." Tina giggled. "Haven't your hands suffered enough?"

The tension broken, they got back to work. Maxim asked Ron, "Are we ready to launch the app?"

Ron gave him a thumbs-up. "Good to go."

Maxim nodded, a strange calm settling over him. "Then we launch."

"You need to see this," Tina called, looking over the edge.

Everyone leaned over the edge of their station, craning to see what Tina was so excited about.

Maxim looked down. He saw the soldiers approach the castle from the outside, and Jean striding toward them from the courtyard.

"Whoa, she's going to take all of them on by herself!" Aleksi gaped. "There's like a hundred of them!"

"Jean could do this before breakfast. Watch and learn, Aleksi." Tina snickered, angling her tablet to get video of the smackdown that was about to occur. "If they weren't here to trash the place and steal from us, I'd almost feel sorry for them. They obviously don't know enough about her to run while they still can."

Jean struck the gates with her armored foot, raising her guns and beginning to fire before they'd even finished clattering open.

Maxim watched as the first salvo annihilated fully ten

percent of the enemy soldiers before they were even aware of what was happening. Soldiers fell left, right, and center as the guns of Jean Dukes sounded their greetings to the intruders.

The sudden decimation shook them, many losing focus as they were sprayed with the fine pink splatter that was all that remained of their brothers- and sisters-in-arms. They were the lucky ones; the ones who were spared the final sight of Saint Payback advancing upon them wearing the hell-hath-no-fury face of the former chief gunnery officer.

Maxim's attention was drawn to a movement in the shadows underneath the rail bridge across the river. "Get on the guns!" he cried. "The bridge. There's somebody under there!"

Craig and Mischa swiveled the mounted guns and fired. The projectiles flew fast and true, slamming into the bridge in a cloud of concrete dust.

A full minute later there was a low **boom** as the supports collapsed in a cloud of dust.

When the dust cleared, the bridge lay twisted and ruined in the river.

"Oh... Oh, *shiiit!*" Craig whispered. "I think we *killed* them."

Maxim shook him. "There is no time for that, my friend. Use your senses; there are more soldiers coming through the trees. We *must* defend the people inside. They are depending on us until John gets back and we can all escape."

Craig turned back to his station, pulling himself together. "You're right, Maxim. I'm sorry."

Maxim chuckled. "Do not be sorry, my friend. Be awesome! You've got this!"

He clapped Craig on the back and moved on to Ron and Aleksi. He found himself enjoying the role of coordinating the group. He'd had no interest in leading day-to-day, but he felt more than alive in the heat of the battle—he felt *awake*. This was where he belonged. "What is the app telling you?" he asked Ron and Aleksi, sliding down the wall to sit between them.

"Here, jump in, but don't touch anything." Ron spoke without looking up and kept typing. Maxim took his tablet out to receive the update. "The satellite is showing multiple bands of enemy troops moving in," Ron told him, "as well as activity from the tanks, but the Pod will take care of them. We can defend this side of the castle, and the Black Eagles will cover the others."

Aleksi chipped in, "We should make it difficult for them. See how the bridge has dammed the river?"

"Uh huh," Maxim said, zooming in on the screen to see where the buildup of churning water was threatening to flood the embankment. "I see. You want to blow the embankment and flood the open area between us and the enemy."

Aleksi nodded. "The mini-missiles should do it."

Maxim jumped up and went to Mischa and Halli. "Did you get all that?"

"*Hells yeah*!" Halli whooped, turning her missile launcher toward the embankment.

"We got it," Mischa declared.

They heard Jean calling from below. "Everything okay up there?"

"Yes!" Maxim replied, peering over. "But you have incoming from the other side of the inlet. We will do our best to slow them down for you."

Jean grinned, her teeth shining in the dark. "You're doing a great job, kids. I'm giving you all an A for this class. Pizza for everyone when we get home!"

They whooped and hollered, and Jean laughed and join in with the eight teenagers dancing around on a castle in the middle of a war.

United Kingdom, North Wales, Conwy Castle Courtyard

Jean applied her size sevens and all her enhanced strength to the gates, firing through the solid oak even as it buckled and slammed open under her determined boot.

Jean looked at the carnage all around her as the gates wobbled to a standstill. She had taken enough of them out with her first volley of shots to make the rest take notice. She let the ones trying to leave get away.

The others she finished as quickly as possible, aware that the kids were watching from the parapet above. She heard them talking between the reports of her pistols, and grinned at the awe in their voices.

The carnage continued as she danced her way through the British soldiers, killing them at a speed they struggled to comprehend. Those who saw her flaked out, shaken to the core by the all-out destruction she caused with a cold smile on her face.

She punctuated her shots with a blistering tirade. "Come to *MY Gott Verdammt* castle, and attack *MY Gott Verdammt* people?" she screamed as they fell. "*My FAMILY?*

Payback's a bitch, you scurvy-ridden pie lovers—*and so am I!*"

Jean was lost in the flow of combat, guided only by muscle memory and raw instinct as the enemy died all around her. A few kept their wits long enough to shoot at her, but she was gone before their rounds left the chamber.

Through the sound of her final shot echoing from the walls behind her, she heard Maxim shout for Craig and Mischa to man the guns. She did a one-eighty, following the streams of projectiles that whizzed over her head toward the rail bridge the Heritage people had given her so much crap about preserving during the planning of this facility.

She clocked the soldiers moving toward her from under the bridge. The kids hadn't done enough damage. She brought her pistols up again and fired six times, taking out the supports completely to ensure that not even one of the approaching enemy soldiers would make it out alive.

The bridge collapsed with a soft *boom*, and she smiled to herself. She'd hated that bridge anyway.

She satisfied herself that the kids were okay after a quick check. If anything, they were running that defense system like pros. She was damn proud of them all for thriving under the pressure. She knew without a doubt that they were going to do great things when they grew up. Or really *stupid* ones, she amended. She still wasn't sure about Craig yet.

Guardians James and Donal had taken the Black Eagles to defend the north and west side, where the castle was abutted by the town in which the facility's employees lived with their families. "Everything okay over there?" she asked, sending to the Black Eagles' comm.

"Nothing on this side, Jean," James reported.

Donal had similar news. "No movement from the tanks, ma'am."

Jean grimaced. "They think this is the weak side, the idiots." She looked up at the battlements, calling to the kids again just as a pair of the mini-missiles launched with a shrieking hiss.

"Whoo!"

She heard them celebrating. "What did you hit?" she yelled.

Tina poked her head over and shouted down, "The embankment on the inlet. It's created a flood plain between the enemy and the castle, but it won't hold them for long."

It didn't hold them at all.

Scores of soldiers came pouring out of the woodland and splashed toward her location, front lines already firing wildly. She was extremely glad for her helmet when a stray round ricocheted off the side of it. The kids let rip with the guns again, the projectiles and random mini-missiles barely making the battle-hardened soldiers pause for thought.

Still they came on, and more came out of the water behind them. She heard a sharp whine, the prelude to a massive explosion in the middle of the soldiers, as Aleksi and Ron activated the laser cannon and razed the ground beneath them.

Dirt rained down, peppered with helmets, rifles, and other—wetter—things.

Jean yelled and raised her guns once more, throwing herself into her work with gusto.

CHAPTER NINETEEN

U nited Kingdom, North Wales, Passenger Pod Over
   River Conwy

John glanced back at Hugh and the children, who had fallen asleep in their father's arms. "You okay?"

Hugh nodded. "I'm fine." His haggard expression and the dark circles under his eyes contradicted his words, though. "I just want to get to Laura. I want it to be over, that's all."

John admired the man's strength. "It'll be over soon," he told him. "We'll take you all up to the *Meredith Reynolds*. You'll be safe there."

The EI cut in as the Pod turned at the mouth of the river, "John, there is a situation at the castle."

He turned back to the console. "Hold our position and bring it up on the viewscreen."

Hugh slid his arms out from under Leo and Lexi and joined John at the console as the Pod halted in midair.

John sucked in a breath when the image appeared. The ground around the castle was lit up with gunfire and small explosions. The bridge lay in the river. He was about to call Jean when the laser beam struck the ground on the southeast side of the castle, scattering soldiers in its wake. "Way to go, kids!" he cheered.

"Kids?" Hugh asked

John's chest swelled with pride. "Yeah, my cousin's kid and her classmates. They're the ones firing that freaking cool laser. I wondered what they were building when I called this afternoon."

Hugh was astonished into silence.

The bright beam threw the battle below into sharp relief. John made out the kids on the parapet wall firing on the scores of soldiers approaching the castle. "Where's Jean?"

"Allow me," the EI said, zooming in on the outside of the castle below the east barbican where John's love slew the enemy in droves.

"That's my Jean," he said fondly.

Hugh looked askance at him, lamenting, "What kind of people did my wife get us involved with? Do you *all* love killing this much?"

John rounded on him. "Who said anything about enjoying killing? What you are seeing is professional pride in a job well done. Every single one of those soldiers is heading for the place with your wife inside, and Jean is standing between her and every single one of them. A bit of gratitude would be nice." He maneuvered the Pod to hover over the spot where Jean was fighting for the lives of the people evacuating the castle.

Hugh spoke apologetically. "I'm sorry, but this is difficult. Nothing like this ever happened around here before TQB arrived."

John tapped a few commands into the console, then locked it and walked to the side door. "I've programmed the Pod to take you three straight to the *Meredith Reynolds*. Don't touch anything. You'll be there shortly, and someone will meet you."

Hugh was taken aback. "What about you?"

John opened the side hatch and put his war face on. "I'll be down there," he said, and jumped out of the Pod, enjoying the shocked expression on Hugh's face as the hatch closed behind him. He touched his comm as he dropped to the ground and opened a channel to Jean. "I'm inbound, babe. Start the evacuation. The Llewellyns are safe."

"About time!" Jean replied. "I'm getting bored down here. They just keep throwing themselves in front of me to die."

He hit the ground with his JD Specials at the ready, bending at the knees to minimize the jarring shock to his spine.

His ears were filled with the resounding thunder of the guns and the whine of the laser cannon, and his vision was filled with Jean in her glory backlit by falling trails of burning debris as Bethany Anne's prototype Pod pucked the continuous artillery fire from the tanks out of the sky.

"Nice superhero landing," she shouted to him over the din. "Glad you could make it. I thought you'd lost your invitation."

He straightened and shot a soldier coming up the bank as he ran toward her. He held out a hand and bowed as he shot another soldier who had gotten too close. "I wouldn't want to miss out on a shindig like this," he replied. "Wanna dance, babe?"

She shot three soldiers in quick succession. "How can I refuse an offer like that?" she deadpanned.

"We have the best date nights." He grinned at her.

They stood back-to-back, turning a deadly circle. The soldiers who mobbed the low slope between the barbican wall and the riverbank died as fast as they came, and eventually they stopped coming completely.

They were almost clear when a helicopter flew in from across the river, followed by two more.

"James and Donal will take care of it," Jean said. "The EI says the evacuation is complete. It's just you, me, and the kids left in the castle. Can you finish up these last few without me? I need to get up to the kids and get our tech dismantled so we can leave."

"Sure thing, babe," John agreed.

As she turned to leave, the weapons on the battlements ceased firing. "*THE KIDS!*" she screamed.

They ran for the battlements at breakneck pace, shooting soldiers as they went.

United Kingdom, North Wales, Battlements, East Barbican

Maxim loaded the last battery of mini-missiles into the launcher for Mischa to fire. "As soon as these are done, strip it and pack it. Like Jean said, we can't leave any TQB tech behind for them to find.

Craig was playing around while he hammered a stand

of trees into matchsticks where he saw movement. *"Pew pew!"*

"Craig, take it seriously!" Tina yelled over the noise.

"Come on!" he yelled back. "This is the coolest thing I've done in my life, and I've been on the moon!"

"You were on the moon for all of two minutes!" Halli snarked. "Just concentrate, Craig. This isn't the time for jokes."

Maxim's tablet vibrated in his hand as he received a notification. "Everyone, keep it together. The evacuation was successful, so we are almost done here."

They were getting ready to wind down their defense when the helicopters flew in. The first two headed straight for the Black Eagles and were shot down by the Guardians. The third veered away at the last second, a lucky reprieve that would not last long.

"It's headed straight for us!" Craig cried.

"Shoot it down!" Mischa screamed as it zoomed toward them. A puck came screaming toward the helicopter, intercepting it moments before it reached the tower—but it was too late.

Four dark shadows swung out on ropes from the open door of the spiraling helicopter and landed on the crenellations at the top of King's tower.

"They're after the weapons," Maxim growled, starting toward the tower as the invaders rappelled down the tower wall on the far side of the parapet.

"They won't get them," Craig snarled, all levity gone from his voice.

"We will fight them. There are more of us than there

are of them," Maxim declared as the assailants reached the bottom and turned toward them, pistols at the ready.

"Do not move," the leader of the men commanded. "If you attempt to rush us, these men, whose teammates you murdered in cold blood, will shoot you full of tranquilizer. I wanted to make it silver after the disrespect you little brats showed to those men, but my bosses had better ideas. Luckily I keep a backup weapon. The first round is lead, but the next is going to hurt a lot more. Are we clear?"

They did a double-take at the man's knowledge of the UnknownWorld.

Maxim glowered at him, a low growl beginning in his throat that was picked up by Craig, Halli, and the twins. They moved as one to surround and protect Tina, Ron and Aleksi, who were crouched by the projectile guns.

"Leave, now," Maxim said coldly, his eyes gleaming yellow. "If you do not listen to this good advice, I cannot be held responsible for what happens to you."

The man sighed and gestured to one of the men, who shot Maxim with a dart, triggering an instant change to his wolf form. He bounded on four legs toward the man, snarling. The other Wechselbalg kids released their inner wolves and flowed over the parapet toward the four men with their own teeth bared.

The men fired over and over, hitting the wolves with dart after dart filled with tranquilizers. The twins went down after the first couple of hits, their wolves being the lightest and smallest of the five. Halli was next after four darts got her in quick succession, leaving Craig and Maxim. The men turned their attention to Maxim, peppering him with darts, and as he went down he saw

Craig fighting the drugs valiantly. He sprang toward the leader, going for the man's throat when the gun went off and Craig flew backwards.

Maxim's eyes drifted shut as the drugs pulled him under.

———

Jean bounded up the narrow stairs to the parapet three at a time, John right behind her as she burst out of the door and saw the men standing over the kids. They raced across the parapet as a man spoke.

"I'm out of tranqs, Agent Broadbent," one of the soldiers said.

"Well, just get the ones we know are werewolves. We have to come out of this with *something*. Sykes, Dawson, give him a hand to get some clothes on them. Good lads."

The soldiers advanced toward the unconscious children, looking at Tina with cold expressions as they bent to grab the clothes Maxim and the others had shed when they changed and began to quickly dress them. They jumped back quickly when Tina came at them. She was the only one of the students still standing. She had a wrench in one hand and a lit welding torch in the other and screamed at them, "Get away from them! *Just you wait until Uncle John gets here!* He's going to kick your asses so hard your great grandkids' great grandkids will have to sit carefully!"

The leader sighed, stepping closer. "You are a tiresome child," he told her. "Give up, you have lost. Our men will *not* have died in vain." He swung his arm up to pistol-whip her into silence.

John was there before his arm had completed its upward arc. He shot Broadbent, blowing a fist-sized hole in the side of his ribcage, his next shots dropping the other three before Broadbent had hit the floor.

He rushed over to Tina, cupping her face and looking into her eyes. "Are you okay?" She broke into sobs and clung to him tightly. He stroked her hair and murmured gently, "It's okay, Teeny. They're dead, they can't hurt you."

"We killed them!"

Jean shook her head. "If you mean the bridge, that was all me."

Tina sighed with relief.

Jean called Bethany Anne's Pod down for pickup as she rushed to tend to the students. She examined the gash Aleksi had opened on his head when a stray tranquilizer dart knocked him out, and gave Ron a wad of cloth to hold over his bleeding nose.

John released Tina and knelt to check the pulses of the sedated Wechselbalg kids, making sure each was steady before moving on to the next.

Craig was covered in blood, but John could find no entry or exit wound. He saw a burn hole in Craig's ragged trousers that he'd missed on his first look. It looked like it had been caused by a bullet, and further inspection revealed a barely healed bullet wound in the boy's leg. John called to Jean, "Craig's been shot in the thigh. It's healing, but we need to get him in the Pod first and get him checked over. I'll bring the others."

Jean picked Craig up and went to wait for the Pod.

Tina clung to John, clearly in shock.

"I'm so proud of you, Tina," he told her as the Pod

descended. "Proud of you all. None of this should have happened, and you kept a cool head throughout. Your mom will be proud, too."

"I was so scared when he pointed his gun in my face!" she exclaimed, bursting into tears again now the danger had passed and her brain began to process the events of the long night.

"Hey, it's all right," John said, enveloping her in a comforting embrace. "I bet he was scared of you, too. What on Earth were you thinking of, taking on men with guns?"

Tina frowned. "That they weren't taking my friends, or our weapons."

John smiled. "You're a pocket rocket, just like your mom." He laughed as a thought struck him. "Hey, Tina?" When she looked up at him, he put on an expression of mock horror for her. "How about we don't tell your mom about *that* part right away. Lead with something less likely to shorten my lifespan instead, okay?"

Tina looked skeptical. "What's she going to do? You're, like, three times her size!"

John gave her a knowing look. "Size means nothing." He shooed her toward the Pod, where Jean was waiting. "Your mom scares the ever-living crap out of me when she's on the warpath."

Tina giggled. "Me too! I'll make sure to tell her how you saved me in the nick of time. That might make her less likely to murder you for this!"

John smiled as she climbed into the Pod on slightly shaky legs. Her shock would pass soon; Tina was smart and strong. He scooped the twins up and carried them into the Pod, placing them gently on the folded-down seats before going back for Maxim and Halli.

Jean closed the hatch when they were all inside the Pod and climbed into the pilot's seat. "Is everyone strapped in?"

"Yeah," John told her. "Let's get out of here."

The Pod lifted off and the castle grew smaller beneath them. "I'll be glad to get home," John remarked. "The sooner we leave this mudball behind for good the better." He watched the ground fall away on the screen, his attention caught by movement. "Hey, Jean, look at them!" He pointed to the swarm of soldiers rushing the castle. "This part always makes me laugh. Why they think we're going to leave any breadcrumbs for them, I don't know."

Tina frowned. "Um, did either of you pick up the crates with the weapons?"

Jean and John looked at each other and shook their heads.

"The *crates*!" Jean spat. She called to the EI, "Stop the Pod. Does this thing have any pucks left?"

"We have two mother-puckers remaining in the arsenal," the EI offered. "Should I deploy them?"

"What are you waiting for?" John demanded. "Mother-*puck* them!"

The screen showed the first mother-pucker slam into King's Tower, knocking massive chunks of stone onto the barbican wall and demolishing it. A second later the second hit the courtyard and smashed through the paving.

Twenty seconds later a flaming crater replaced the castle. "That ought to do it," he quipped. "Shame about the castle."

Tina began laughing and clapped her hands over her mouth to stifle it.

"What's so funny?" John asked.

"Nothing, just…" She snorted again. "You're not going to get this past Diane and Dorene. They're going to skin you both alive when we get back. This was worse than the moon incident *and* the Great Wall disaster rolled into one!"

"She's right," Jean admitted. "We're going to get it in the neck for this."

John made a face. "At least the Ds are afraid of you. *I'll* be the one getting strips torn off me."

Jean patted him on the arm. "As long as they keep their hands off your behind, my love, I'm fine with it!"

CHAPTER TWENTY

Q BBS *Meredith Reynolds*, Etheric Academy
Administration Office

Diane and Doreen spat fire at the Queen.

Bethany Anne sat calmly opposite the apoplectic sisters, nodding and listening as they ranted.

"This can't go on." Diane scowled. "Every time one of them takes our students off the *Meredith Reynolds,* they put their lives at risk. The Great Wall situation was bad enough, but having them take part in a full-scale battle? We've come to you because it's gone too far!"

"Not to mention those idiotic fighter jocks taking *their* students out for live fire exercises! Someone could have been killed!" Dorene banged her hand on the desk. "No more learning in the field until we get it through the thick heads of the faculty that they are responsible for *children,* not redshirt interns!"

The Queen rested her chin on her folded hands as she considered their words. "So what are you saying...that the Academy isn't working?"

Diane shook her head. "No, we're saying that the *faculty* isn't working. With the notable exception of your father, almost every single one of them has neglected to protect their students in one way or another. We want them fired from their teaching roles and restricted to keeping the curriculum up to date." She crossed her arms resolutely.

Dorene interjected, "It can be done. There was a good mix of professionals and families among the last three thousand immigrants, and we will schedule a new intake exam once they have all settled in. The current structure is too loose to keep everything running smoothly…" She paused and looked at her sister when she saw the faraway expression on the Queen's face.

"Is she even still here with us?" Diane whispered out of the side of her mouth.

She jumped in her seat when Bethany Anne fixed her with narrowed eyes.

"Yes, I'm still here. I've reviewed the records, and I agree with you both. What are your suggestions for fixing the issues?"

Diane and Dorene had all the answers.

"Fire them all."

"Stop allowing the students to go gallivanting around on Earth."

"We need a more traditional structure, with the enriching and nurturing environment we planned when we started this."

"Get us some *qualified* teachers."

They shouted the final demand in unison. "*AND NO MORE ENDANGERING THE STUDENTS!*"

The Queen leaned forward slightly. "You're telling me that the only problem is the faculty?"

Diane snorted. "Have you *seen* the video of Jean from the castle?"

Bethany Anne grinned. "You know I have."

Diane's expression was colder than ice. "And you don't think it was *inappropriate* for Jean to allow the students to participate in that battle? She let them operate an untested experimental *Gott Verdammt* laser!" She took a breath to calm herself before resuming in a softer tone. "They're still just children, Bethany Anne. They will have a lifetime to experience the reality of our world. They shouldn't be exposed to that at school."

Dorene had the final say, although she kept her voice respectful. "And you shouldn't have okayed the students being present during the siege at the castle." She flinched, expecting a rebuke for speaking to the Queen so boldly.

Bethany Anne shrugged. "I think they did just fine, but you're right. Check your tablets, ladies. I had ADAM send over the files of possible teaching candidates."

Dorene opened her tablet, took a quick look through the list, and nodded in satisfaction. "There will have to be a break in classes while we arrange interviews and get the new faculty up to speed."

The Queen nodded, getting up from the chair. "After everything the kids have just been through down there they could probably *use* a break. Call it midyear vacation or something. Make it so. *But,*" she twirled a finger to emphasize the point, bringing it to rest on the two of them with a wicked smile, "*you* can deal with the firing part yourselves. They'll be waiting for you in the auditorium in an hour."

Diane and Dorene gaped as the Queen disappeared.

"We have to fire them?" Dorene's eyes glinted dangerously.

Diane's face became mischievous. "I have a better idea." She wrote a sentence on a piece of paper and slid it across the desk toward her sister.

Dorene read the piece of paper and cracked up. "You just *love* riling them up, don't you?"

"It's my mission in life, DJ," she managed to squeeze out through her own gales of laughter. "Anyway, today we get to tear Jean a new one. You can't say you're *not* looking forward to it!"

Dorene wiped away her tears. "Oh, you know I am! How about we go and get dinner after we finish laying down the law? There's a certain young Wechselbalg who is still in possession of all of his limbs, so I believe you owe me a steak."

Diane grasped her chest in mock shock. "You owe *me*! I bet he would get injured, not that he would lose a limb."

Dorene scowled, then laughed. "Yeah, but he got shot being heroic. I think we'll call it a draw." She sobered. "You don't think it's too soon for Craig to graduate?"

"No." Diane shook her head. "I agree with Peter. He's ready for the structure the Guardians will give him. He's growing up, DJ."

"They all are," Dorene replied wistfully.

CHAPTER TWENTY-ONE

QBBS *Meredith Reynolds*, Etheric Academy, Auditorium

There was an air of nervousness among the assembled faculty.

John folded his arms across his chest and extended his legs into the aisle next to the uncomfortable chair. "I feel like I'm back in detention," he grumbled to Jean, who sat beside him in the next seat.

"Me too," she agreed.

"You and me both," Bobcat chimed in simultaneously from the other side of Jean. "We're grown-ass adults. We shouldn't be summoned like school kids who got caught playing hooky."

Marcus and William sidled in through the back door and took seats at the back near Isaac, making that every faculty member present except the General and Admiral Thomas.

"I can sympathize." A handsome blond man in a pilot

uniform said, leaning over from the row behind. "What are you all in for?"

Bobcat hung his head. "Busted fair and square this time. I had a couple of the kids working on something in the brewery."

Jean shook her head. "That'll do it. What about you, Thomas?"

The blond man pursed his lips. "Took the students out to shoot up asteroids. I don't even know why they have a problem with it. Those kids are almost as sharp as us regular pilots," he complained. "Why are you two here? Weren't you down on Earth?"

Jean glanced at John. How to begin? "Um…"

Diane and Dorene walked out onto the stage. The conversation was over.

The Academy administrators halted at the edge of the stage and glared down at all of them with equal amounts of anger and disappointment. They let the silence drag out, making the audience itch under the scrutiny. The tension ratcheted up with every passing second.

Finally Dorene spoke. "This Academy was founded on the principle that our best and brightest children would be given a safe environment in which to learn and grow. You have been called here today because, in one regard or another, you have failed to provide that environment for your students." She stalked back and forth across the stage, pointing at Thomas and Bobcat in turn. "Your days of endangering the students are over! Dogfights in space, irresponsibility and questionable moral influence." She changed course abruptly and turned on Jean and John. *"You two* used a full-blown siege as a *Gott Verdammt* training exercise!"

Jean bristled as a murmur went around the assembled faculty. She stood up to defend the kids. "Which they all passed with flying colors! I don't see the issue. These kids are heading for this life. We should be preparing them for it as best as we can." She sat down again with a thump, folded her arms, and glared back at the two administrators.

Diane stepped forward, her voice dripping disdain. "If this is the best you can do, I won't feel as bad about what I have to say next. Your teaching days are *over*."

Bobcat let out a whoop, clapping his hand over his mouth when the icy stares of the twins zeroed in on him. "Sorry, ma'am," he muttered.

"You're not getting away that easily, you boob!" Doreen snarled. "And it's not all about your complete inability to keep those kids out of the Medical wing either." Her voice softened just a little. "The Empire is expanding. New arrivals bringing their families means *more* students. The Academy's focus is shifting to classroom-based learning to accommodate this growth."

Diane took over. "Three thousand people have just arrived on the *Meredith Reynolds*, and their children are eligible for a place at the Academy if they can pass the entrance exam. We cannot expect you to provide a well-rounded education for them all on top of all your other duties in the run-up to our departure through the Gate. You are the spine of the Empire —the hands that build it and the shepherds who protect us. But while you are the font of all our knowledge, you're just too damn *stupid* when it comes to the safety of the students!"

She swung her finger in an arc to point at everyone present. "I said your *teaching* days were over, but I didn't say you were absolved of your responsibility to the Academy. Every single one of you is being promoted. Congratulations, you are all now Dean of your department."

"Dammit!" Bobcat exclaimed.

Diane glared at him. "When you've quite finished? You are going to come up with material that can be learned and then taught by the new instructional staff. Do not leave out a *single thing* that the students on track for your specialty need to learn to succeed in their futures."

"Because their future is the future of the whole Empire," Dorene finished.

Jean smiled to herself. The twins might have thought this was a punishment, but as far as she was concerned it was a much better role. She waved a hand in the air to get attention. "When will you have the new faculty lined up?"

"Dorene is arranging candidate interviews. You'll sit in on the interviews, and then the best candidates will shadow you as part of their retraining."

Isaac called out. "Retraining? Why?"

Diane clapped. "Good question. It's good to see that there's at least one thinker among you. How many of you were there when this Academy was dreamed up?" Hands went up. "Do you remember *why* this school was supposed to be different?"

"Because the old system didn't work," John said so quietly only Jean could hear him.

Diane continued, "The public education system—the one found in schools all across the Earth—is broken. The brightest are held back, while those needing extra support are left behind. Teachers have given up, and have stopped believing in the value of their vocation." She sighed. "*This* is what we need to change. While they have the relevant qualifications to be able to teach, many of the candidates have come from the public education systems around the world. Their *mindset* is what we need to retrain. We need to help them rediscover the reason they chose to teach in the first place, before the system knocked their ideals and enthusiasm out of them."

There were nods and murmurs of agreement from everyone seated.

Dorene waved her hands to quiet them. "Enough of your chin-wagging. The future depends on what we pass on for future generations. The students that come through this Academy are our *legacy*, and the hope for everyone's future. Now, get your backsides out of here and put together the best *Gott Verdammt* curriculum that has ever been created!"

CHAPTER TWENTY-TWO

Q BBS *Meredith Reynolds*, Etheric Academy, Cafeteria

"Is that cheese I smell?" Tina's mouth watered as she joined the others at the table. "Happy graduation, Craig!" She held up a hand to high-five him.

"Thanks, Tina," Craig replied cheerfully.

Chef Van came out of the kitchen carrying a stack of steaming pizza boxes. "Courtesy of Jean Dukes," he said as he deposited a pizza in front of each student. "Meat, meat, and beets for my favorite Wechselbalg kids. Hawaiian for Aleksi. Veggie-plus for my man Ron. Last but not least, the ultimate cheese feast for Tina."

"Thanks, Chef Van!" they chorused.

Tina opened her box and breathed in the heavenly aroma. "Mmmm, you got the Bay Grill recipe!" The pizza filled the box from corner to corner, and there were at least five types of cheese, judging by the colors.

"I added my own touch, if you are wondering. There

are *seven* different cheeses. Enjoy!" Chef Van winked and went back to the kitchen.

"Meat, meat, and beets?" Craig asked, hesitating over his first slice.

"Try it, is good," Maxim said through a mouthful of pizza.

Craig took a bite and chewed gingerly. "No way! It *is* good!"

Maxim chortled, folding the rest of his slice so he could fit more in his mouth. "Listen to me. I am a wise friend."

"I'm going to miss your sound advice," Craig mused. "What's a veggie-plus?" he asked Ron.

"It's a vegetarian supreme with pepperoni," Ron revealed. "Want to try some?" He pushed the box toward Craig, who accepted a slice eagerly.

"It is true you are going to the Guardians?" Nestor asked as Craig took a bite.

Craig nodded. "Peter said it was time, now that I've settled down a bit." He took a bite of his pizza just as Maxim smacked him across the back heartily in celebration.

"Ewww!" Mischa cried as the blob of half-chewed food hit the table. "You boys are gross!

He snagged it with a napkin and continued, "I was nervous when I went to meet the guys I'll be training with, but they're all cool."

"You *will* remember us when you're a mighty Guardian, won't you?" Mischa joked.

Yana entered the cafeteria with Bai Hu trailing behind. She headed straight for the table and the pizza boxes, and snagged each of them a slice before sliding onto the bench next to Tina. "It is so good to eat together again. Come and sit." she gestured to Bai Hu. "Have you all met my new little brother yet?"

Bai Hu blushed and looked down with curiosity at the pizza Yana had handed to him. "Hello," he mumbled shyly.

"It's great to see you, Bai Hu," Ron said. "Are you settling in okay with Yana and Nicholas?"

Bai Hu's face lit up. "They are my family now. Yana is a good *jiějiě.*"

"That means 'big sister,'" Yana clarified for the group, pulling Bai Hu into a one-armed hug. "I have been learning to speak Mandarin as my little brother here learns English. He is a much faster learner than I am, though."

"You are doing well," Maxim encouraged the younger boy. "We also had to learn to speak English when we arrived. You will get it in no time."

Bai Hu blushed deeper. "I try new words every day. My tablet tells me what I want to know. I think it was magic at first, but it is Meredith who is magic."

This brought a friendly laugh from them all and Bai Hu blushed again, unused to the attention.

"She sure is," Aleksi agreed. He went quiet for a moment. "I will miss *this* when the break is over and our new classes start."

"We have a few weeks before that." Craig tried to mollify him.

It didn't work—Aleksi still looked glum. "Yes, but after that we go back to our own classes. I have enjoyed getting to know you all better."

"Even if it was in the middle of a warzone?" Masha

quipped. "I'm sure we can arrange another if it would make you happy."

Craig fell about laughing at that, setting off a chain reaction which spread through them like a virus. One by one they succumbed, until even little Bai Hu, who only had a faint idea of what was happening, was rolling about with the infectious mirth.

Ron managed to speak through his tears. "Sure, let's do that!"

Tina clutched her stomach. "Oh my... Can't breathe..."

"I'm glad we are back together," Yana said when they'd pulled themselves together. "But I also enjoyed this time apart, even if I did not believe I would. I made friends of Ksenia and Jayden, and I learned a lot from Tina's mom. She showed me enough that I know what I want to do when we graduate."

"What are you going to do?" Maxim asked, head tilted in curiosity. "I have also seen my future."

Yana clasped her hands together in glee. "I'm going to focus on cultural relations and diplomatic studies. I want to meet the new species and learn about them. Help make the road to becoming allies smooth, starting with the Yollins. What about you?"

Maxim grinned. "I realized exactly where my heart lies during the battle at the castle. I will fight to protect our people against those who do not wish to be our allies. As soon as Commander Silvers will allow it, I am enlisting in the Guardians."

Craig clapped him on the back. "That's great, buddy! I'll look out for you when you get there."

"That would be good, my friend." He looked thoughtful

for a moment. "Perhaps I have learned the value of accepting others too, Yana."

"God help the enemy when *you* grow up, Maxim. You did a great job of leading us through the siege." Aleksi grinned. "When you go to war, I will be in your ear directing. I knew I would be headed for tactical, anyway. Everything that happened at the castle just confirmed that for me."

"And I will be flying high above, defending you from the skies of whatever planets we visit," Nestor put in.

"You all seem so certain of the future," Mischa fretted. "We still have time to decide, right? School isn't over yet."

Tina reached over and patted her hand. "You don't have to know yet. I haven't decided for sure what I want to do and I don't intend to just yet, either. You two don't graduate until the year after us, so there's plenty of time to decide what to specialize in."

"I already know what I will do." Masha smirked. "I will be a spy, and sneak about getting information to help the Empire after we go through the Gate."

Ron grinned. "*Now* all your illicit skills make sense! I'm going to work for Ms. Dukes' department. I had an idea for armor that I want to develop into something real."

"Who knows what the future holds?" Tina speculated, looking around the table at her closest friends. "We've only just begun to discover what we are capable of."

FINIS

Thank you!!! And you!!! And *you*, too!!!!

Book! ... Book! ... Book!

Oh wait, we just *had* the book! Thank you so much for reading it! It wasn't that long ago that I was in the Fans and Authors group on Facebook baying for this book along with the rest of you. Now, *WOW!* I was the one blessed with bringing it to you! For those of you who aren't familiar with my admin posts from Fans Write, settle in. This is going to be long, soppy, and in UK English (sorry, JIT!) I am Welsh, after all.

I almost cried when I heard that Scott (TS) Paul was having so much success with his Federal Witch series that he (quite rightly) was prioritizing it over Alpha Class. Okay, I cried... Just a little bit... Ok, I cry all the time, but that's neither here nor there. I was *sad*, like we all were! When Michael asked me if I'd like to take over, it took me less than a fraction of a second to reply, "YES! OF COURSE!!!" This was the book that got left behind, and we just don't do that around here!

I need to talk about Fans Write first, because without it you wouldn't have this book at all. If you don't know the story, eight or so months ago I decided to be brave and take Michael up on the offer he made in *his* Authors Notes. It went something like, "hey, want to come and do some writing?" (at least that's what *I* read) so I reached out, and Fans Write was born. Just after New Year's 2018 Volume I hit the 'Zon and not a single one of the authors involved expected the overwhelmingly positive reaction from everyone who read it, or the strong friendships that formed between us as a result. We *did* expect it to get bigger, though, and we were right! Volume II is underway with plans for Vol-III and Vol-IV in place. (Popping my admin hat on for a second... if you have an idea for a TKG fanfic, come and join us, there's a link at the end of my notes)

I can't tell you all how overwhelmed I am by all the support from our wonderful community after Fans Write Vol-I was released. Thanks to all of you, I get to write in the *best* universe in the history of universes for the *best* fans in the history of fans! So thank you! I raise my patented Guaranteed TKG Author Motivator (pitchfork) in salute to you all!

I dedicated this book to everyone who has been right alongside me as I made the journey from fan to author, because I don't have the words to express how much it means to me to have you all cheering in my corner. So for all my family, friends, and everyone I've met in the last few months who has been there—*you are amazing*!

Special mentions for Micky Cocker, James Caplan, and Kelly O'Donnell for all the time they spent with me in

January helping me improve every aspect of my writing. You all are too modest! I had a serious level-up, both in skill and speed, and that's reflected in Discovery. You rock, and I love you all! (Editor's note: she really did! This book is amazing!) Edit from Nat: This book is even more awesome because Lynne is magic.

Another edit from Nat: JIT did a fantastic job of picking out every tiny little thing. They were the maths teacher who looks at your sums and says "Where's your working out?" and it made a big difference. Thank you all!

Much respect to Diane and Dorene (the real ones) for allowing me a glimpse into their minds. I'm utterly in awe of you both, and my snark game improves every time we talk!

Massive love to Lynne Stiegler and Steve Campbell for making this story into the polished book I know it will be by release day. Lynne, you're an absolute legend and I *love* when you send me cute animal memes (especially when I should be writing!). Steve, you have an answer for every question and you never think I'm silly for asking!

Let's all admire Jeff the Artist for this cover as well, it's so cool! I was unsure of the process, and you pulled this out of the bag. Fabulous!

Huge thanks to Karla Kay for the priceless resource that is the wiki. Seriously, it saved me SO many times!

Last but not least, my fantastic co-author (who I'm going to embarrass now, see the next bit to find out why) Working with Michael is the most amazing experience! He's going to laugh at this, but it's kind of like I went to see The Beatles, and John Lennon invited me up on stage to sing *Imagine* and then passed me the mic and told me to make up my own verse. I sat writing Bethany Anne and realised mid-sentence that this is the *canon* I'm writing and my hands just *shook*. That is a gift I will be eternally grateful for. He says it will sink in, but I hope it never does and I get to keep my sense of wonderment forever.

Being an Author

It's really cool over on the author side of things. Slack is like an office that I don't have to get dressed to go to, and everyone there talks about books all day and night. It's author heaven! Sarah (SE) Weir, Erika Everest and I have been furiously plotting (books, not world dominance) over in our Slack channel and I can tell you that you're going to *love* what they are bringing you! If you would like to find out what they are up to, pop along to our Facebook group, STARDUST (link at the bottom)

Slack is fun, except when it's almost 2am and I'm squinting at the screen and MA is *punking* me! (Editor's note: he does that!) See the evidence...

(*very* late chat on Slack)

MA: So, what's your date? ;)

(biiig long pause while I open and close my mouth like a fish—my brain is fried because I've been editing Discovery nonstop for the entire day!)

MA: (Steve helps w/ dates)

Nat: Cool. I went blank then ;)

MA: <snicker>

Nat: *narrows eyes*

Joking aside, it is an absolute joy and my honour to work with you, Michael. You are nurturing, kind, and a *hell* of a lot of fun! I couldn't ask for a better co-author to begin my writing career with. I learn something new every time we talk, and I *love* that! Here's to many more books together!

Alpha Class (and beyond!)

Writing *Discovery* was both a challenge and a dream come true. The challenge was to bring you a continuation of the story that *I* (as a rabid pitchfork-wielding superfan) would be happy with, and to do it in four weeks or less. I think this is the best thing I've written yet, and book four is going to be even better!

My favourite bit in *Discovery* is the scene where Jean Dukes storms out of the gates at the beginning of the siege. I sent a snippet to Erika and Sarah, and Erika coined the phrase 'delicate dismemberment' to describe my writing style—which I love, and have adopted.

I am *dying* to know what the community thinks about the direction I've taken Alpha Class in! Come and find me and tell me! I'll put links to all the TKG groups I hang out in at the end and I'm getting an author page together right now that should be up and running by the time you read this (reviews are nice too, thank you in advance if you take the time to leave one after you're done reading!). If I'm not writing, I'm on Facebook, talking!

Uh-oh, I can hear the chant starting again! When will Alpha Class book four be ready? I'm starting it next week, and you can expect a fun story to close out the arc. I've been having the most fun planning it, and I'm looking forward to getting you all involved. After that I'll be getting to work on *Holi's War*, the continuation of my first story in FWVI. You demanded it, so it shall be!

Until then,

Ad Aeternitatem,

Nat

P.S. Here are the links I promised, I hope I see you there!

My author page
https://www.facebook.com/NDRobertsBooks/
STARDUST: Stories by the Sisters Three
https://www.facebook.com/groups/414869612270799/?
source_id=1808528092775135
Kurtherian Gambit Fans Write for the Fans group https://
www.facebook.com/groups/TKGFansWrite/
Kurtherian Gambit Group for Fans and Authors https://
www.facebook.com/groups/AgeofExpansion/

First, THANK YOU for not only reading our story, but reading these author notes as well!

I'm not too sure where to start with this story.

(I'm sitting in a PF Chang's restaurant in Henderson, NV right now. Somewhere around here lives the military sci-fi author Richard Fox– I'll have to ask him sometime when it doesn't seem like I'm being a stalky-stalker.)

Ok, back to starting again. I guess I could go back to the last thing I was thinking a moment ago about Natale's journey.

It was the way she ended her author notes "Ad Aeternitatem." You might recognize that phrase from earlier books in the Kurtherian Gambit Universe, and something I started placing at the end of my author notes (I was thinking of Stan Lee's "Excelsior!" when I started doing that.)

Now my co-authors are writing it! I am getting such a kick out of seeing their names in print, and the love and fun they are enjoying.

Last summer I was dreaming up new ways to get the word about Kurtherian Gambit out to other readers, and the BEST marketing is word-of-mouth. Or for couples, "giggles-of mouth" work really well. You know, when one of you giggles at 2:00 o'clock in the morning and your partner who is trying to sleep is woken up because you laughed out loud at one of our books?

Yeah, *that's* the best marketing.

Anyway, I was thinking about the blessings in my life, and the coolness of how many of my fans who have taken the plunge to become authors. The challenge was, SO many of you have reached out with story ideas, but they couldn't / can't go anywhere for legal reasons with me.

Yet 20BooksTo50k (Facebook group I started) was too much for many of the fans who, like me, aspired to write something and be published. What could I do?

These thoughts and a couple of others swirled in my head, and I created that offer in the Author Notes so long ago which Natale decided to go for. I'll let her tell you more of the story—but suffice it to say that because of you, the fans, allowing me the opportunity to share with you, *a person in another country has found her calling!*

She is an author!

I am very aware how blessed I am. I am very aware the gift you provide me, and I am honored to provide said gift (opportunity) to others.

What I was NOT aware of, and it continues to amaze me, is the willingness of so many of you to join the Kurtherian Fans Write for the Fans group and help others who aspire to write. You do it as beta readers, JIT readers, support fans and everything else.

You are changing lives, which brings me back to Natale.

Her life was changed when that first TKG Fans Write anthology was published. She has found friends in other countries who will be with her for years. She is supported by caring folks whose passion is reading, and who are just awesome human beings. Without YOU, her life would have absolutely taken a different path.

Now, I think you can tell from her author notes and support that she is loving every day, and her family's life will be affected positively because "we" readers *give a shit* and we are willing to offer a chance to new authors in a safe environment.

Many of you congratulate me on finding them and having great co-authors.

Folks, I'd love to take credit for some amazing smarts or something, but finding Natale, (Erika, Sarah and the others) was a damned fluke.

I don't think I thought about how cool it would be to find new authors who already know the Universe and are passionate about writing in it. I didn't stop to consider the ramifications of *GROWING* the collaborators through the book series.

In hindsight, it is stupidly obvious—but that's *hindsight*.

Now, Natale is the first out of the gate as the 'second wave' of fans becoming authors. I'd put TS (Scott) Paul as the very first wave, and arguably the most famous due to his own work.

(Technically Paul C. Middleton was the first to write in TKG – but I'm speaking to the first fan to publish a book.)

So, I think it is very appropriate that the first of the second generation takes the baton here on Book 03 of the

Etheric Academy from the first of the previous generation and closes out the series.

So, welcome her to The Kurtherian Gambit Universe the way we do all of our freshman authors—with a Review where you ask...

"WHERE'S THE NEXT ONE?"

Ad Aeternitatem,

Michael Anderle

Jack Dalton Book 7

Jack Dalton Book 8

Jack Dalton Book 9

Jack Dalton Book 10

Magical Division Origins

Jack Dalton, Monster Hunter Box Set (1-3)

Jack Dalton, Monster Hunter Box Set (4-6)

Jack Dalton, Monster Hunter Box Set (7-10)

Jack Dalton Monster Hunter: The Complete Collection (Books 1-10)

Athena Lee Chronicles

The Forgotten Engineer

Engineering Murder

Ghost Ships of Terra

Revolutionary

Insurrection

Imperial Subversion

The Martian Inheritance - Audio Now Available

Infiltration

Prelude to War

War to the Knife

Ghosts of Noodlemass Past

Forgotten Hope

Athena Lee Universe

Shades of Learning

Space Cadets

The Federal Witch: The Collected Works, Book 1

Chronicles of Athena Lee Book 1-3

Chronicles of Athena Lee Book 4-6

Chronicles of Athena Lee Book 7-9 plus the prequel

New Beginnings

Kutherian Gambit

Alpha Class. The Etheric Academy book 1

Alpha Class - Engineering. The Etheric Academy Book 2

The Etheric Academy (2 Book Series)

WANT MORE KURTHERIAN GAMBIT?

Join the Kurtherian Gambit email list here: http://kurtherianbooks.com/email-list/

Join the Kurtherian Gambit Facebook Group Here: https://www.facebook.com/TheKurtherianGambitBooks/